3|3|

MAID FOR THE MILLIONAIRE

MAID FOR THE MILLIONAIRE

SUSAN MEIER

MILLS & BOON

First published in Great Britain 2010
by Mills & Boon, an imprint of HarperCollins*Publishers*
1 London Bridge Street, London, SE1 9GF

Large Print edition 2018

ISBN: 978-0-263-07448-2

MIX
Paper from
responsible sources
FSC™ C007454

This book is produced from independently certified
FSC™ paper to ensure responsible forest management.
For more information visit www.harpercollins.co.uk/green.

Printed and bound in Great Britain
by CPI Group (UK) Ltd, Croydon, CR0 4YY

Special thanks to Denise Meyers,
who lets me talk out my ideas…

CHAPTER ONE

PINK UNDERWEAR?

Grimacing, Cain Nestor tossed his formerly white cotton briefs into the washing machine and slammed the door closed. Damn it! He should have stopped at the mall the night before and bought new ones, but it had been late when his private plane finally landed in Miami. Besides, back in Kansas he had done his own laundry plenty of times. He couldn't believe he'd forgotten so much in twelve years that he'd end up with pink underwear, but apparently he had.

Tightening the knot of the towel at his waist, he stormed out of the laundry room and into the kitchen just as the back door opened. From the pretty yellow ruffled apron that was the trademark of Happy Maids, he knew that his personal assistant, Ava, was one step ahead of him again. He'd been without a housekeeper since the beginning of February, three long weeks ago. Though Ava had interviewed, he'd found something wrong with every person she'd chosen—his maid lived in and a man couldn't be too careful about whom he let stay in his home—but the lack of clean underwear had clearly proven he'd hit a wall.

Leave it to his assistant to think of the stopgap measure. She'd hired a cleaning service.

Ready to make an apology for his appearance, Cain caught his once-a-week housekeeper's gaze and his heart froze in his chest. His breathing stopped. His thigh muscles turned to rubber.

"Liz?"

Though her long black hair had been pulled into a severe bun at her nape and she'd lost a few pounds in the three years since he'd seen her, he'd know those catlike green eyes anywhere.

"Cain?"

A million questions danced through his head, but they were quickly replaced by recriminations. She'd quit a very good job in Philadelphia and moved with him to Miami when she'd married him. Now, she was a maid? Not even a permanently employed housekeeper. She was a fill-in. A stopgap measure.

And it was his fault.

He swallowed. "I don't know what to say."

Liz Harper blinked a few times, making sure her eyes were not deceiving her and she really was seeing her ex-husband standing wrapped in only a towel in the kitchen of the house that was her first assignment for the day. He hadn't changed a bit in three years. His onyx eyes still had the uncanny ability to make her feel he could see the whole way to her soul. He still wore his black hair short. And he still had incredible muscles that rippled when he moved. Broad shoulders. Defined pecs. And six-pack abs. All of which were on display at the moment.

She licked her suddenly dry lips. "You could start by saying, 'Excuse my nakedness. I'll just run upstairs and get a robe.'"

Remarkably, that made him laugh, and myriad memories assaulted her....

The day they'd met on the flight from Dallas to Philadelphia...

How they'd exchanged business cards and he'd called her cell phone even before she was out of the airport...

How they'd had dinner that night, entered into a long-distance relationship, made love for the first time on the beach just beyond his beautiful Miami home, and married on the spur of the moment in Las Vegas.

And now she was his housekeeper.

Could a woman fall any farther?

Worse, she wasn't in a position where she could turn down this job.

"Okay. I'll just—"

"Do you think—"

They stopped. The scent of his soap drifted to her and she realized he hadn't changed brands. More memories danced through her head. The warmth of his touch. The seriousness of his kiss.

She cleared her throat. "You first."

He shook his head. "No. Ladies first."

"Okay." She pulled in a breath. She didn't have to tell him her secrets. Wouldn't be so foolish again as to trust him with her dreams. If everything went well, she wouldn't even have to see him while she did her job. "Are you going to have a problem with this?"

He gripped his towel a little tighter. "You working for me or chatting about you working for me while I stand here just about naked?"

Her cheeks heated. The reminder that he was naked under one thin towel caused her blood to simmer with anticipation. For another two people that might be ridiculous three years after their divorce, but she and Cain had always had chemistry. Realistically, she knew it wouldn't simply disappear. After all, it had been strong enough to coax a normally sensible Pennsylvania girl to quit her dream job and follow him to Miami, and strong enough that a typically reclusive entrepreneur had opened up and let her into his life.

"Me working here for you until you hire a new maid." She motioned around the kitchen. The bronze and tan cut-glass backsplash accented tall cherrywood cabinets and bright stainless-steel appliances. "Is *that* going to be a problem?"

He glanced at the ceramic tile floor then back up at her. "I've gotta be honest, Liz. It does make me feel uncomfortable."

"Why? You're not supposed to be here when I am. In fact, I was told you're usually at the office by eight. It's a fluke that we've even run into each other. And I need this job!"

"Which is exactly why I feel bad."

That changed her blood from simmering with chemistry to boiling with fury. *"You feel sorry for me?"*

He winced. "Not sorry, per se—"

"Then sorry, per what?" But as the words tumbled out of her mouth she realized what was going on. Three steps got her to the big center island of his kitchen. "You think I fell apart when our marriage did and now I can only get a job as a maid?"

"Well—"

Three more steps had her standing in front of

him. "Honey, I *own* this company. I am the original Happy Maid."

She was tall enough that she only had to tilt her head slightly to catch his gaze, but when she did she regretted it. His dark eyes told her their closeness had resurrected their chemistry for him, too. Heat and need tightened her insides. Her breathing stuttered out of her chest. The faint scent of soap she'd sniffed while at the door hit her full force bringing back wonderful, painful memories.

He stepped away and broke eye contact. "Nice try."

"Call your personal assistant." When her voice came out as a breathy whisper, Liz paused and gulped some air to strengthen it. "I'm the one she dealt with. I signed the contract."

"If you're the owner, why are *you* cleaning my house?" He stopped. His sharp black eyes narrowed. "You're spying."

"On you? Really? After three years?" She huffed out a sound of disgust and turned away, then whirled to face him again. "You have got to be the most vain man in the world! I was hired through your assistant. She didn't give me your name. She hired me to clean the house of the CEO of Cain Corporation. I never associated you with Cain Corporation. Last I heard your company name was Nestor Construction."

"Nestor Construction is a wholly owned subsidiary of Cain Corporation."

"Fantastic." She pivoted and walked back to the center island. "Here's the deal. I have six employees and enough work for seven. But I can't hire the people I need and work exclusively in the office until I get enough work for eight." She also wouldn't tell him that she was scrambling to employ every woman from A Friend Indeed, a charity that provided temporary housing for women who needed a second chance. He didn't understand charities. He most certainly didn't understand second chances.

"Then my profit margins will allow me to take a salary while I spend my days marketing the business and the expansions I have planned."

"Expansions?"

"I'm getting into gardening and pool cleaning." She combed her fingers through the loose hair that had escaped the knot at her nape. "Down the road. Right now, I'm on the cusp with the maid service. I seriously need thirty more clients."

He whistled.

"It's not such a stretch in a city like Miami!"

"I'm not whistling at the difficulty. I'm impressed. When did you get into this?"

She hesitated then wondered why. It shouldn't matter. "Three years ago."

"You decided to start a company after we divorced?"

She raised her chin. She would not allow him to make her feel bad for her choices. "No. I took a few cleaning jobs to support myself when I moved out and it sort of blossomed."

"I offered you alimony."

"I didn't want it." Squaring her shoulders, she caught his gaze. Mistake. She'd always imagined that if she ever saw him again, their conversation would focus on why she'd left him without a word of explanation. Instead the floodgates of their chemistry had been opened, and she'd bet her last cent neither one of them was thinking about their disagreements. The look in his dark eyes brought to mind memories of satin sheets and days spent in bed.

"In a year I had enough work for myself and another maid full-time. In six more months I had four employees. I stayed level like that until I hit a boom again and added two employees. That's when I realized I could turn this business into something great."

"Okay, then."

"Okay?"

"I get it. I know what it's like to have a big idea and want to succeed." He turned away. "And as you said, our paths won't cross."

"So this is really okay?"

"Yeah. It's okay." He faced her again with a wince. "You wouldn't happen to be doing laundry first, would you?"

"Why?"

"I sort of made fifty percent of my underwear pink."

She laughed, and visions of other times, other laughter, assailed her and she felt as if she were caught in a time warp. Their marriage had ended so badly she'd forgotten the good times and now suddenly here they were all at the forefront of her mind. But that was wrong. Six years and buckets of tears had passed since the "good times" that nudged them to get married the week they'd accompanied friends to Vegas for their elopement. Only a few weeks after their hasty wedding, those good times became few and far between. By the time she left him they were nonexistent.

And now she was his maid.

"Is the other fifty percent in a basket somewhere?"

"Yes." He hooked a thumb behind him. "Laundry room."

"Do you have about an hour's worth of work you can do while you wait?"

"Yes."

"And you'll go to your office or study or to your bedroom to do that."

"I have an office in the back."

"Great. I'll get on the laundry."

A little over an hour later, Cain pulled his Porsche into the parking space in front of the office building he owned. He jumped out, marched into the lobby and headed for the private elevator in the back. He rode it to the top floor, where it opened onto his huge office.

"Ava!"

He strode to his desk, dropping his briefcase on the small round conference table as he passed it. He'd managed not to think about Liz as she moved around his home, vacuuming while the washing machine ran, then the dryer. To her credit, she hadn't sauntered into his office and dumped a clean pair of tidy-whities on the document he was reviewing. She'd simply stepped into the room, announced that the laundry had been folded and now sat on his bed. But it was seeing the tidy stack on his black satin bedspread that caused unwanted emotions to tumble through him.

When they were married she'd insisted on doing laundry. She hadn't wanted a maid. She had stayed home and taken care of him.

As he'd stared at the neat pile, the years had slid away. Feelings he'd managed to bury had risen up like lava. She'd adored him and he'd worshipped her. He hadn't slept with a woman before her or one since who had made him feel what Liz could. And now she was in his house again.

Which was wrong. Absolutely, totally and completely wrong. For a woman who'd adored him and a man who'd worshipped her, they'd hurt each other beyond belief in the last year of their marriage. She hadn't even left a note when she'd gone. Her attorney had contacted him. She hadn't wanted his money, hadn't wanted to say goodbye. She simply wanted to be away from him, and he had been relieved when she left. It was wrong—wrong, wrong, wrong—for them to even be in the same room! He couldn't believe he'd agreed to this, but being nearly naked had definitely thrown him off his game.

Underwear in his possession, he had dressed

quickly, thinking he'd have to sneak out, wondering if it would be prudent to have Ava call her and ask her to assign another of her employees to his house. But as she promised, she was nowhere to be seen when he left.

"Just a bit curious, Ava," he said when his short, slightly chubby, fifty-something-assistant stepped into his office. "Why'd you choose Happy Maids?"

She didn't bat an eye. "They come highly recommended and they're taking new clients." She peered at him over the rim of her black frame glasses. "Do you know how hard it is to get a good maid in Miami?"

"Apparently very hard or I'd have one right now."

"I've been handling my end. It's you who—" Her face froze. "Oh." Her eyes squeezed shut. "You were there when the maid arrived, weren't you?"

"Naked, in a towel, coming out of my laundry room."

She pressed her hand to her chest. "I'm so sorry."

He studied her face for signs that she knew Liz was his ex-wife, but her blue eyes were as innocent as a kitten's.

"I should have realized that you'd sleep late after four days of traveling." She sank to the sofa just inside the door. "I'm sorry."

"It's okay."

"No. Seriously. I am sorry. I know how you hate dealing with people." She bounced off the sofa and scampered to the desk. "But let's not dwell on it. It's over and it will never happen again." Changing the subject, she pointed at the mail on his desk. "This stack is the mail from the week. This stack is the messages I pulled off voice mail for you. This stack is messages I took for you. People I talked to." She looked up and smiled. "And I'll call the maid and tell her not to come until after nine next week."

"She's fine." She was. Now that his emotions were under control again, logic had kicked in. The fact that she wasn't around when he left the house that morning proved she didn't want to see him any more than he wanted to see her. If there was one thing he knew about Liz, it was that she was honest. If she said he'd never see her, she'd do everything in her power to make it so. That, at least, hadn't changed. Though she was the one to leave, the disintegration of their marriage had been his fault. He didn't want to upset her over a non-problem. He'd upset her enough in one lifetime.

"No. No. Let me call," Ava chirped happily. "I know that you don't like to run into people. You don't like to deal with people at all. That's my job, remember?"

"I can handle one maid."

Her expression skewed into one of total confusion. "Really?"

The skepticism in her voice almost made him want to ask her why she'd question that. But she was right. Her job was to keep little things away from him. Not necessarily people, but nitpicky tasks. It was probably a mistake that she'd said people. But whatever the reason she'd said it, it was irrelevant.

"I won't have to deal with her. I'll be out of my house by seven-thirty next week. It won't be a problem."

"Okay." She nodded eagerly, then all but ran from the room.

As Cain sank into his office chair, he frowned, Ava's words ringing in his head. Had it been a mistake when she said she knew he didn't like dealing with people or was he really that hard to get along with?

Once again, irrelevant. He got along just fine with the people he needed to get along with.

He reached for the stack of mail. All of it had been opened by Ava and sorted according to which of his three companies it pertained to. He read documents, correspondence and bids for up-coming projects, until he came to an envelope that hadn't been opened.

He twisted it until he could read the return address and he understood why. It was from his parents. His birthday had come and gone that week.

Of course, his parents hadn't forgotten. Probably his sister hadn't, either. But he had.

He grabbed his letter opener, slit the seal and pulled out four inches of bubble wrap that protected a framed picture. Unwinding the bubble wrap—his dad always went a bit overboard—he exposed the picture and went still.

The family photo.

He leaned back in his chair, rubbed his hand across his chin.

The sticky note attached to the frame said, *Thought you might like this for your desk. Happy birthday.*

He tried to simply put it back in the envelope, but couldn't. His eyes were drawn to the people posing so happily.

His parents were dressed in their Sunday best. His sister wore an outfit that looked like she'd gotten it from somebody's trash—and considering that she'd been sixteen at the time, he suspected she might have. Cain wore a suit as did his brother, Tom, his hand on Cain's shoulder.

"If you get into trouble," Tom had said a million times, "you call me first. Not Mom and Dad. I'll get you out of it, then we'll break the news to the wardens."

Cain sniffed a laugh. Tom had always called their parents the wardens. Or the guards. Their parents were incredibly kind, open-minded people, but Tom loved to make jokes. Play with words. He'd had the type of sense of humor that made him popular no matter where he went.

Cain returned the picture to its envelope. He knew what his dad was really saying when he suggested Cain put the picture on his desk. Six years had gone by. It was time to move on. To remember in a good way, not sadly, that his older brother, the kindest, funniest, smartest of the Nestors, had been killed three days before his own wedding, only three weeks after Cain and Liz had eloped.

But he wasn't ready.

He might never be.

CHAPTER TWO

"ARE YOU KIDDING ME?" Carrying boxes of groceries up the walk to the entrance of one of the homes owned by A Friend Indeed, Ellie "Magic" Swanson turned to face Liz. Her amber-colored eyes were as round as two full moons.

"Nope. My first client of the day was my ex-husband."

She hadn't meant to tell Ellie about Cain, but it had slipped out, the way things always seemed to slip out with Ellie. She was a sweet, smart, eager twenty-two-year-old who had gotten involved with the wrong man and desperately needed a break in life. Liz had given her a job only to discover that it was Liz who benefited from the relationship more than Ellie did. Desperate for a second chance, Ellie had become an invaluable employee. Which is why Liz didn't merely provide cleaning services and grocery delivery services for A Friend Indeed, she also tried to give a job to every woman staying at the shelter homes who wanted one. She firmly believed in second chances.

Ellie shouldered open the back door, revealing the outdated but neat and clean kitchen. "How can that happen?"

"His assistant, Ava, hired us to clean the house of the CEO of Cain Corporation."

"And you didn't know your ex-husband was CEO of Cain Corporation?"

Liz set her box of groceries on the counter. "When we were married he only owned Nestor Construction. Apparently in three years he's branched out. Moved to a bigger house, too." In some ways it hurt that he'd sold the beach house they'd shared, but in others it didn't surprise her. He'd been so lost, so despondent after the death of his brother, that he'd thrown even more of himself into his work than before. The much larger house on the beach had probably been a reward for reaching a goal.

Ellie walked out of the pantry where she had begun storing canned goods, her beautiful face set in firm lines and her long blond curls bouncing. "I'll take his house next week."

"Are you kidding? He'll think I didn't come back because I was intimidated." She pointed her thumb at her chest. "I'm going. Besides, I have something else for you." She opened her shoulder-strap purse and rifled through its contents. After finding the employment application of a young woman, Rita, whom she'd interviewed the night before, she handed it to Ellie.

"What do you think?"

"Looks okay to me." She glanced up. "You checked her references?"

"Yes. But she's staying at one of our Friend Indeed houses. I thought you might know her."

Ellie shook her head. "No."

"Well, you'll be getting to know her next week. As soon as we're through here, we'll drop by the house she and her kids are using and tell her she's got the job and that she'll be working with you."

"You want me to train her?"

"My goal is to get myself out of the field and into the office permanently." Such as it was. The desk and chairs were secondhand. The air-conditioning rarely worked. The tile on the floor needed replacing. The only nice features of the crowded room were the bright yellow paint on the walls and the yellow-and-black area rug she'd found to cover most of the floor. But she was much better off than the women who came to A Friend Indeed, and working with them kept her grounded, appreciative of what she had, how far she'd come. It wasn't so long ago that her mom had run from her abusive father with her and her sisters. The second chance they'd found because of a shelter had changed the course of not just her mom's life, but also her life and her sisters'.

"To do that, I have to start teaching you to be my new second in command."

Pulling canned goods from the box on the counter, Ellie glanced up again.

Liz smiled. "The promotion comes with a raise."

Ellie's mouth fell open and she dropped the

cans before racing to Liz to hug her. "I will do the best job of anybody you've ever seen!"

"I know you will."

"And seriously, I'll take your ex-husband's house."

"I'm fine. My husband wasn't abusive, remember? Simply distant and upset about his brother's death." She shrugged. "Besides, our paths won't cross. We'll be fine."

Liz reassured Ellie, but she wasn't a hundred percent certain it was true. Though she and Cain wouldn't run into each other, she'd be touching his things, seeing bits and pieces of his life, opening old wounds. But she needed the job. A recommendation from Cain or his assistant could go a long way to getting the additional clients she needed. She wanted to expand. She wanted to be able to employ every woman who needed a second chance. To do that, she had to get more business.

Liz and Ellie finished storing the groceries and made a quick sweep through the house to be sure it was clean. A new family would be arriving later that afternoon to spend a few weeks regrouping before they moved on to a new life.

Satisfied that the house was ready for its new occupants, Liz led Ellie through the garage to the Happy Maids vehicle. The walk through the downstairs to the garage reminded her that she was content, happy with her life. She was smarter now and more confident than she had been when she was married. Surely she could handle being on the periphery of Cain's life.

The following Friday morning when it was time to clean Cain's house again, she sat in the bright yellow Happy Maids car a few houses down from Cain's, telling herself it wouldn't matter what she found. If the cupboards were bare, she wouldn't worry about whether or not he was eating. She would assume he was dining out. If his mail sat unopened, she'd dust around it. Even if there were lace panties between the sheets, she would not care.

Fortified, she waited until he pulled his gorgeous black Porsche out of his driveway and headed in the other direction. But just as their encounter the week before had brought back memories of happier times, seeing him in the Porsche reminded her of their rides along the ocean. With the convertible top down. The wind whipping her hair in all directions.

She squeezed her eyes shut. Their marriage had been abysmal. He was a withdrawn workaholic. Though his brother's death had caused him to stop talking almost completely, she'd seen signs that Cain might not be as involved in their relationship as she was during their six-month courtship. Canceled plans. Meetings that were more important than weekends with her. It had been an impulsive, reckless decision to marry. When she was his girlfriend, he at least tried to make time for her when she visited from Philadelphia. When she became his wife, he didn't feel the need to do that and she'd been miserably alone. When they actually did have time together, he'd been antsy, obviously thinking about his company and the work he could be doing. He'd never even tried to squeeze her into his life. So why wasn't she remembering that?

Fortified again, she slid the Happy Maids car into his drive and entered his house. As she'd noticed the week before, there were no personal touches. No pictures. No awards. No memorabilia.

Glancing around, she realized how easy it would be to pretend it was the home of a stranger. Releasing any thought of Cain from her mind and focusing on doing the best possible job for her "client," she cleaned quickly and efficiently. When she was done, she locked up and left as if this job were any other.

The following week, she decided that her mistake the Friday before had been watching him leave for work, seeing him in "their" beautiful Porsche. So she shifted his house from the first on her list to the second, and knew he was already gone by the time she got there. As she punched that week's code into the alarm to disable it and unlocked the kitchen door, she once again blanked her mind of any thought of Cain, pretending this was the house of a stranger.

Tossing the first load of laundry into the washer, she thought she heard a noise. She stopped, listened, but didn't hear it again. She returned to the kitchen and didn't hear any more noise, but something felt off. She told herself she was imagining things, stacked dishes in the dishwasher and turned it on.

She spent the next hour cleaning the downstairs in between trips to the laundry room. When the laundry was folded, she walked up the cherry-wood staircase to the second floor. Humming a bit, happy with how well she was managing to keep her focus off the house's owner, she shouldered open the master bedroom door and gasped.

Damn.

"Who is it?"

The scratchy voice that came from the bed didn't sound like Cain's at all. But even in the dim light of his room, she could see it was him.

"It's me. Liz. Cleaning your house."

"Liz?"

His weak voice panicked her and she set the stack of clean laundry on the mirrored vanity and raced to the bed. His dark hair was soaked with sweat and spiked out in all directions. Black stubble covered his chin and cheeks.

"My *wife*, Liz?" he asked groggily.

"Ex-wife." She pressed her hand to his forehead. "You're burning up!"

Not waiting for a reply, she rushed into the master bathroom and searched through the drawers of the cherrywood vanity of the double sinks looking for something that might help him. Among the various toiletries, she eventually found some aspirin. She ran tap water into the glass and raced back to the bed.

Handing two aspirin and the water to him, she said, "Here."

He took the pills, but didn't say anything. As he passed the water glass back to her, he caught her gaze. His dark eyes were shiny from the effects of the fever, so she wasn't surprised when he lay down and immediately drifted off to sleep again.

She took the glass downstairs and put it in the

sink. Telling herself to forget he was in the bedroom, she finished cleaning but couldn't leave ‑
in good conscience without checking up on him.

When she returned to the bedroom, Cain still
slept soundly. She pressed her hand to his forehead again and frowned. Even after the aspirin,
he was still burning up and he was so alone that
it felt wrong to leave him. She could call his assistant but somehow that didn't seem right, either. An assistant shouldn't have to nurse him
through the flu.

Technically an ex-wife shouldn't, either, but
with his family at least a thousand miles away in
Kansas, she was the lesser of two evils.

Sort of.

Tiptoeing out of the room, she pulled her cell
phone from her apron pocket and dialed Ellie.

"Hey, sweetie," Ellie greeted her, obviously
having noted the caller ID.

"Hey, Ellie. Is Rita with you?"

"Sure is. Doing wonderfully I might add."

"That's good because I think I need to have her
take over my jobs this afternoon."

"On her own?"

"Is that a problem?"

Ellie's voice turned unexpectedly professional. "No. She'll be great."

"Good."

"Um, boss, I know where you are, remember? Is there anything going on I should know about?"

"No. I'm fine. I just decided to take the afternoon off." Liz winced. She hadn't actually lied. She was taking time off; she simply wasn't going to do something fun as Ellie suspected.

"No kidding! That's great."

"Yeah, so I'll be out of reach for the rest of the day. Give the other girls a call and instruct them to call you, not me, if they have a problem."

"On it, boss!" Ellie said, then she laughed. "This is so exciting!"

Liz smiled, glad Ellie was enjoying her new responsibilities. "I'll see you tomorrow."

She closed her cell phone then ambled to the kitchen. She'd promised herself she wouldn't care if he had food or not, but with him as sick as he was, he had to at least have chicken broth and orange juice. Finding neither, she grabbed her purse and keys and headed to the grocery store where she purchased flu medicine, orange juice, chicken broth and a paperback book.

She put everything but the flu meds and book away, then she grabbed a clean glass from the cupboard and tiptoed upstairs again. He roused when she entered.

"Liz?"

"Yes. I have flu meds. You interested?"

"God, yes."

"Great. Sit up."

She poured one dose of the flu meds into the little plastic cup and held it out to him. He swallowed the thick syrup and handed the cup back before lying down again.

As she took the medicine to the bathroom, a bubble of fear rose up in her. Caring for him had the potential to go so wrong. Not because she worried that they'd get involved again. Tomorrow, she would forget all about this, if only because even pondering being involved with him would bring back painful memories.

But she knew Cain. He hated owing people, and if she stayed too long or did too much, he'd think he owed her. When he believed he owed somebody he could be like a dog with a bone. Being beholden made him feel weak. He was never weak. Which made her caring for him when he was sick a double threat. Not only had he been weak, but she'd seen him weak. He'd *have* to make this up to her.

Of course, with him as sick as he was, she could hope he wouldn't remember most of this in the morning.

Everything would be fine.

With a peek at the bed to be sure he was asleep, she left the room and went to the Happy Maids car. In the trunk, she found a pair of sweatpants and a tank top. She changed out of her yellow maid uniform in one of the downstairs bathrooms then she took her book and a glass of orange juice into the study. Reclining on the sofa, she made herself comfortable to read.

She checked on him every hour or so. Finding him sleeping soundly every time, she slid out of the room and returned to the study. But just as she was pulling the door closed behind her on the fourth trip, he called out to her.

"Where are you going?"

She eased the door open again and walked over to the bed. "Cain? Are you okay?"

"I'm fine." He sat up. "Come back to bed."

Realizing the fever had him hallucinating or mixing up the past and present, she smiled and went into the bathroom to get him some water. She pressed the glass to his lips. "Sip."

As she held the glass to his mouth, he lifted his hand to the back of her thigh and possessively slid it up to her bottom.

Shock nearly caused her to spill water all over him. She hadn't even dated since she left him, and the feeling of a man's hand on her behind was equal parts startling and wonderful.

He smiled up at her. "I'm better."

Ignoring the enticing warmth spiraling through her, she tried to sound like an impartial nurse when she said, "You're hallucinating."

His hand lovingly roamed her bottom as his

fever-glazed eyes gazed up at her longingly. "Please. I seriously feel better. Come back to bed."

His last words were a hoarse whisper that tip-toed into the silent room, the yearning in them like a living thing. She reminded herself that this wasn't Cain. The Cain she'd married was a cold, distant man. But a little part of her couldn't help admitting that this was the man she'd always wished he would be. Loving. Eager for her. Happy to be with her. ✓

Which scared her more than the hand on her bottom. Wishing and hoping were what had gotten her into trouble in the first place—why she'd married him that impulsive day in Vegas. On that trip, he'd been so loving, so sweet, so happy that she'd stupidly believed that if they were married, if she didn't live a thousand miles away, they wouldn't have to spend the first day of each of their trips getting reacquainted. He'd be comfortable with her. Happy.

And for three weeks they had been. Then his brother had died, forcing him to help his dad run the family business in Kansas through e-mails and teleconference calls, as he also ran Nestor Construction. Their marriage had become one more thing in his life that he had to do. A burden to him.

That's what she had to remember. She'd become a burden to him.

She pulled away, straightening her shoulders. She wasn't anybody's burden. Not ever.

"Go back to sleep."

She returned to the study and her book, but realized that in her eagerness to get out of the room she'd forgotten to give him another dose of medicine. So she returned to his room and found him sleeping peacefully. Not wanting to disturb him, she took a seat on the chair by the window. The next time he stirred, she'd be there to give him the meds. She opened her book and began to read in the pale light of the lamp behind her.

Cain awakened from what had been the worst night of his life. Spasms of shivers had overtaken him in between bouts of heat so intense his pillow was wet with sweat. He'd thrown up. All his muscles ached. But that wasn't the half of it. He'd dreamed Liz had taken his temperature, given him medicine and walked him to and from the bathroom.

With a groan, he tossed off the covers and sat up in bed. He didn't want to remember the feeling of her palm on his forehead, the scent of her that lingered when she had hovered over him or the wave of longing that swept through him just imagining that she was back in his life. He pulled in a breath. How could he dream about a woman who'd left him without a word of explanation? A woman who was in his bed one day and gone without a word the next?

Because he'd been a fool. That's how. He'd lost her because he was always working, never had time for her, and grieving his brother. No matter how she'd left, he couldn't blame her. She was innocent of any wrongdoing...and that was why he still wanted her.

As his eyes adjusted, he noticed soft light spilling toward him from across the room. He must have left the bathroom light on. He looked to the left and saw Liz watching him from his reading chair.

He licked his dry lips. She was so beautiful. Silhouetted in the pale light from the bathroom, she looked ethereal. Her long black hair floated around her, accenting her smooth, perfect alabaster skin. She wore sweatpants and a tank top, and he realized she'd turned off the air-conditioning. Probably because of his shivering.

Still, her being in his bedroom didn't make sense. They'd divorced three years ago.

"Why are you here?" he demanded. "*How* are you here?"

"I'm your maid, remember?"

"My maid?"

"Your assistant hired Happy Maids to clean your house once a week—"

He closed his eyes and lay down again, as it all came back to him. "Yeah. I remember."

"You were pretty sick when I got here Friday morning."

"Friday morning?" He sat up again and then

groaned when his stiff muscles protested. "What day is it?"

"Relax. It's early Saturday morning."

He peered over. "You've been here all night?"

She inclined her head. "You were very sick. I didn't feel comfortable leaving you."

He fell back to the pillow. "Honest Liz."

"That's why hundreds of people let me and my company into their homes every week to clean. My reputation precedes me."

He could hear the smile in her voice and fought a wave of nostalgia. "I guess thanks are in order."

"You're welcome."

"And I probably owe you an apology for fondling your butt."

"Oh, so you remember that?"

This time she laughed. The soft sound drifted to him, smoothed over him, made him long for everything he'd had and lost.

Which made him feel foolish, stupid, *weak*. She was gone. He had lost her. He could take total blame. But he refused to let any mistake make him weak.

"You know what? I appreciate all the help you've given me, but I think I can handle things from here on out."

"You're kicking me out?"

"I'm not kicking you out. I'm granting you a pardon. Consider this a get-out-of-jail-free card."

"Okay." She rose from the chair. Book under her arm, she headed for the door. But she stopped and glanced back at him. "You're sure?"

He'd expect nothing less from her than absolute selflessness. Which made him feel like an absolute creep. He tried to cover that with a smile so she wouldn't even have a hint of how hard just seeing her was for him. "I'm positive. I feel terrific."

"Okay."

With that she opened the door and slipped out. When the door closed behind her, he hung his head. It had been an accident of fate that he'd gotten the flu the very day she was here to clean his house. But he wasn't an idiot. His reaction to her proved that having her back in his life—even as a temporary employee—wasn't going to work.

The weeks it took Ava to find a permanent maid would be filled with a barrage of memories that would overwhelm him with intense sadness one minute and yearning for what might have been the next.

He should get rid of her. That's what his common sense was telling him to do. But in his heart he knew he owed her. For more than just staying with him while he was sick. He should have never talked her into marrying him.

CHAPTER THREE

IT WAS FIVE O'CLOCK when Liz finally fell into bed. Ellie called her around eleven, reminding her that they were taking Amanda Gray and her children, the family who had moved into the Friend Indeed house the weekend before, to the beach.

She slogged out from under the covers and woke herself up in the shower. She pulled a pair of shorts and a navy blue-and-white striped T-shirt over her white bikini, and drove to Amanda's temporary house. Ellie's little blue car was already in the driveway. She pushed out into the hot Miami day and walked around back to the kitchen door.

"Mrs. Harper!" Amanda's three-year-old daughter Joy bounced with happiness as Liz entered and she froze.

Liz had been part of the welcoming committee when Amanda and her children had arrived at the house, but until this very second she hadn't made the connection that Joy was about the age her child would have been.

Her child.

Her heart splintered. She should have a child right now. But she didn't. She'd lost her baby. Lost her marriage. Lost everything in what seemed like the blink of an eye.

Swallowing hard, she got rid of the lump in her throat. The barrage of self-pity that assailed her wasn't just unexpected; it was unwanted. She knew spending so much time with Cain had caused her to make the connection between her baby and Joy. But that didn't mean she had to wallow in it. Her miscarriage had been three years ago. She'd had therapy. She might long for that child with every fiber of her being, but, out of necessity, she'd moved on.

Amanda, a tall redhead with big blue eyes, corrected her daughter. "It's Ms. Harper, not Mrs."

"That's okay," Liz said walking into the

kitchen, knowing she had to push through this. If she was going to work in the same city as her ex, she might not be able to avoid him. She most definitely couldn't avoid all children the same age her child would have been. Being in contact with both might be a new phase of her recovery.

She could handle this. She *would* handle this.

"Smells great in here."

"I made French toast," Ellie said, standing at the stove. "Want some?"

"No. We're late." She peeked into the picnic basket she'd instructed Ellie to bring. "When we get to the beach, I'll just eat some of the fruit you packed."

"Okay." Ellie removed her apron and hung it in the pantry. "Then we're ready to go."

Amanda turned to the hall. "I'll get Billy."

Billy was a sixteen-year-old who deserted them the second the two cars they drove to the beach stopped in the public parking lot. Obviously expecting his desertion, Amanda waved at his back as he ran to a crowd of kids his own age playing volleyball.

Amanda, Ellie and Liz spent the next hours building a sand castle with Joy who was thrilled with all the attention. Around four o'clock, Ellie and Amanda left the sand to set up a picnic under their umbrella.

Joy smiled up at Liz. "Do you like sand?"

She gazed down at the adorable cherub. The wind tossed her thin blond locks. Her blue eyes sparkled. Now that Liz was over the shock of realizing Joy and her baby would have been close to the same age, she felt normal again. Strong. Accepting of that particular sadness in her life. That was the difference between her and Cain. She'd dealt with her loss. She hadn't let it turn her into someone who couldn't connect with people.

"I love the beach. I'm happy to have someone to share it with."

Joy nodded enthusiastically. "Me, too!"

They ate the sandwiches and fruit Ellie had packed for dinner, then Joy fell asleep under the umbrella. Obviously relaxed and happy, Amanda lay beside her daughter and closed her eyes, too.

"So what did you do yesterday?" Ellie singsonged in the voice that told Liz she knew something out of the ordinary had happened the day before.

Liz peered over at Ellie. Did the woman have a sixth sense about everything? "Not much."

"Oh, come on. You never take a day off. I know something happened."

Liz grabbed the bottle of sunscreen and put her attention to applying it. Knowing Ellie wouldn't let her alone unless she told her something, she said, "I was taking care of a sick friend."

Ellie nudged her playfully. "So? Who was this friend?"

"Just a friend."

"A man!"

"I said nothing about a man."

Ellie laughed. "You didn't need to. The fact that you won't give me a name or elaborate proves I'm right."

How could she argue with that?

Ellie squeezed her shoulder. "I'm proud of you."

"Don't make a big deal out of it."

Ellie laughed gaily. "Let's see. You not only

took a day off, but you were with a man and I'm not supposed to make a big deal out of it?"

"No, you're not. Because I'm never going to see him again."

"How do you know?"

"Because I know."

"Okay, then." Ellie closed her eyes and her face scrunched comically.

"What are you doing?"

"Wishing that you'd see him again."

"You might not want to do that."

"Oh, I think I do."

"The man was my ex."

Ellie's eyes popped open. "Oh, Liz! Damn it. You should have told me that before I wished. You know how powerful my wishes can be."

"That's why I told you now. You need to take it back."

"I can't."

"Yeah, well, you'd better or you're going to break your record of wishes granted. Because I'm not going to see him again."

Stupidly, that made her sad. She'd loved Cain

with her whole heart and soul, but his brother had died and he'd gone into his shell. She'd tried to hang in there with him, to be there when he reached the point that he could work through his pain and withdrawal, but he never had. And then one day she realized she was pregnant. She knew in her heart that Cain wasn't ready for a child, so she'd waited a few weeks, hoping that if she were further along the pregnancy would seem more real to him. Maybe even be a cause for joy.

But she'd miscarried before she'd had a chance to tell him and suddenly she was the one unable to function. She knew she needed help. At the very least she needed someone to talk to. She couldn't talk to Cain. She wouldn't have been able to handle it if he had dismissed the loss of the little life so precious to her. So she'd gone. Their marriage had been in shambles anyway. The miscarriage simply pointed out what she already knew. Cain wasn't emotionally available.

Ending their marriage had been the right thing to do. She'd gotten therapy, moved on and made a wonderful life for herself.

And he'd moved on. Achieved the success he'd always wanted.

There was nothing to be sad about.

She spent most of the rest of the day in the ocean with Joy, until all thoughts of her miscarriage and her ex-husband had receded. Through the week, occasionally something would remind her of her short pregnancy or her doomed marriage, but she ruthlessly squelched the urge to feel sorry for herself until by Friday, she didn't have a second thought about going to Cain's house to clean. The past was the past. She'd moved on, into the future.

Assuming he'd already gone to work, Liz simply pulled the Happy Maids car into his driveway, bounced out and let herself into his kitchen.

But when she turned from pulling her key from the door, she saw Cain standing over a tall stack of waffles.

"Good morning."

She froze.

They weren't supposed to run into each other. That was why she thought she could keep this job. But three of her four cleaning trips to his house, he'd been home. Without even knowing it, he'd dredged up memories that she'd had to deal with. Emotions she'd thought long dead. Now here he was again.

Still, she wouldn't make an argument of it. She could say a few words of casual conversation, as she walked to the door on the other side of the kitchen and slipped out of the room to clean another section of the house.

"You must be really hungry."

He laughed. "I am. But these are for you." He shrugged. "A thank-you for helping me last weekend."

She froze. She should have expected this. She *had* expected this. She knew he hated owing anyone.

She sucked in a quiet breath. Not only did she not want to spend time with him, but she hadn't eaten waffles since their fateful trip to Vegas. Mostly because she didn't want to remember that wonderful time. *That* Cain wasn't the real Cain. Neither was this guy who'd made her waffles.

He didn't want to thank her as much as he felt guilty that she'd helped him the week before and wouldn't let that "debt" go unpaid.

"That's not necessary."

"I know it's not necessary, but I *want* to thank you."

"You did thank me. The words are enough."

He sighed. "Just sit down and have a waffle."

"No!" Because the single word came out so angrily, she smiled to soften it. "Thanks, but no."

Their gazes held for a few seconds. She read the confusion in his dark eyes. He didn't understand why she wouldn't eat breakfast with him. They'd been so happy the one and only time they'd had waffles together. And maybe that's why he'd chosen them?

Regret rose up in her, but regret was a foolish emotion. She couldn't change who he was. She couldn't change the fact that she'd lost their child. And she refused to be pulled into believing the nice side of him was in control. That would only lead to more heartache. Neither one of them wanted that.

She turned and walked away. "I'll get started upstairs while you eat."

Cain pretended her refusal to eat his thank-you waffles hadn't bothered him. Being incredibly busy at work, it was easy to block out the memory. But Saturday morning he took his boat out, and alone on the water with nothing to keep him company but his thoughts, he was miserable.

Liz was without a doubt the kindest woman in the world and he had hurt her. He'd hurt her enough that she couldn't even force herself to be polite and eat breakfast with him.

When she'd left him three years before, he'd experienced a bit of remorse, but mostly he was relieved. He'd quickly buried both emotions under work—as he always did. But sitting on the ocean, with the sun on his face and the truth stirring his soul, he knew he had to make it up to her. All of it. The quick marriage, the horrible three years together, the bitter divorce and probably the pain she'd suffered afterward.

He owed her. And he hated owing anyone. But

her refusal had shown him that she didn't want a grand gesture. Hell, she didn't want any gesture at all. Still, he needed to ease his own conscience by doing something for her. And he would. He simply wouldn't let her know he was doing it.

On Sunday morning, he got her phone number from Ava and tried calling her. He needed no more than a ten-minute conversation with her. He was very, very good at figuring out what people wanted or needed. That was part of what had made him so successful at negotiating. In ten minutes, he could figure out what anyone wanted or needed and then he could use that knowledge to negotiate for what *he* wanted. The situation with Liz was no different. He wanted to ease his conscience and could do that by simply finding a need and filling it for her. Anonymously, of course. Then his conscience would be clear. He could fall out of her life again, and they both could go back to the new lives they'd created without each other.

His call went directly to voice mail, so he tried calling her on Monday morning. That call also went to voice mail. Not wanting to make a fool of himself by leaving a hundred unanswered messages, he waited for Friday to roll around. She might not take his calls, she might not have eaten the breakfast he'd prepared the week before, but she couldn't avoid him in his own house if he really wanted to talk to her.

And he did. In only a few minutes, he could ascertain what was important to her, get it and ease his conscience. If he had to follow her around while she dusted, he would.

Realizing she might not enter if she saw he was still home, Cain stayed out of sight until he heard the bip, bip, bip of his alarm being disabled. He waited to hear the back door open and close, then he stepped into the kitchen.

"Liz."

The woman in the yellow maid's apron turned. "Mr. Nestor?"

"Oh, I'm sorry."

Well, if that didn't take the cake! Not only had she refused his thank-you waffles and ignored his calls, but now she'd sent someone else to clean his house?

He sucked in a breath to control his temper so he could apologize again to Liz's employee, then he drove to his office. He was done with pussyfooting around. Now, she'd deal with him on his terms.

He kept the five o'clock space on his calendar open assuming she and her employees met back at her office for some sort of debriefing at the end of the work week. At the very least, to get their weekly paychecks. Ava gave him the business address she'd gotten for Happy Maids and he jumped into his black Porsche.

With traffic, the drive took forty minutes, not the twenty he'd planned on. By the time he arrived at the office building housing Happy Maids, he saw a line of women in yellow aprons exiting. He quickly found a parking place for his car, but even before he could shut off his engine, Liz whizzed by him in an ugly green car.

Damn it!

Yanking on the Porsche's gearshift, he roared

out of the parking space. He wasn't entirely sure it was a good idea to follow Liz home. She might take that as an invasion of privacy, but right at this moment, with the memory of her refusal to eat his waffles ringing in his head, and his embarrassment when he realized she'd given the job of cleaning his house to one of her employees adding fuel to the fire, he didn't give a damn.

He wanted to get this off his conscience and all he needed was ten minutes. But she wouldn't even give him ten minutes. So he'd have to take them. He wasn't sure how he'd explain his presence at her door, but he suddenly realized he had the perfect topic of conversation. He could calmly, kindly, ask her why she'd left their marriage without a word. Three years had gone by. The subject wasn't touchy anymore. At least not for him. He knew why she'd left. He'd been a lousy husband. This should be something she'd want to discuss. To get off her chest.

He wouldn't be mean. He'd say the words women loved to hear. That he wanted to talk. To clean their slate. For closure. So they could both move on completely. Actually, what he was doing was giving her a chance to vent. She'd probably be thrilled for it.

He grinned. He was a genius. Mostly because Liz was the kind of woman she was. She didn't rant and rail. Or even get angry. She'd probably quietly tell him that she'd left him because he had been a nightmare to live with, and he would humbly agree, not argue, showing her he really did want closure. All the while he'd be processing her house, looking for clues of what mattered to her, what she needed. So he could get it for her and wipe this off his conscience.

He wove in and out of traffic two car lengths behind her, not surprised when she drove to one of Miami's lower-middle-class neighborhoods. She identified with blue-collar people. Which was one of the reasons their marriage had been so stressful. She'd been afraid to come out of her shell. Afraid of saying or doing the wrong thing with his wealthy friends. Afraid, even, to plan their own parties.

She pulled her car onto the driveway of a modest home and jumped out. As she ducked into the one-car garage and disappeared, he drove in behind her.

He took a second to catch his breath and organize his thoughts. First he would apologize for being presumptuous when he made the waffles for her. Then he'd give her the spiel about wanting a clean slate—which, now that he thought about it, was true. He was here to help them move on. Then he'd do what he did best. He'd observe her surroundings, really listen to what she said and figure out what he could do for her.

Taking a few measured breaths, he got out of his car and started up the cracked cement sidewalk. He was amazingly calm by the time a little girl of about three answered the door after he rang the bell.

"Mom!" she screamed, turning and running back into the dark foyer. "It's a stranger!"

Cain blinked. His mouth fell open. Then his entire body froze in fear. Liz had a child? A child old enough to be...well, *his?*

Oh, dear God. That would explain why she'd left without a word. Why she'd avoided him—

Liz and a red-haired woman Cain didn't recognize raced into the hall leading to the foyer. The red-haired woman pushed the little girl behind her in a move that very obviously said this was her child, not Liz's.

Chastising his overactive imagination, Cain forced his breathing back to normal but it wasn't so easy to get his heart rate off red alert.

And Liz still barreled up the hall, looking ready for a fight. She was only a few feet in front of him before she recognized him.

"Oh. It's you." Sighing heavily, she turned to the redhead. "This is my ex-husband, Cain."

Still coming down from the shock of thinking he was a dad, he quickly said, "I'm here to apologize about the waffles last week."

"Apology accepted. Now leave."

Wow. She was a lot quicker on her feet than he'd remembered. "No. I can't. I mean, you didn't have to send another employee to clean my house today." Embarrassment twisted his tongue. He wasn't saying any of this well. Where was the control that helped him schmooze bankers, sweet-talk union reps and haggle with suppliers?

Gone. That's where. Because Liz wasn't a banker, union rep or supplier. She was a normal person. His ex-wife. Now he understood Ava's comments the day he'd discovered Liz was his temporary maid. He wasn't good at ordinary conversation with ordinary people. Business was his element. That was why he didn't have a personal life.

Still, he needed to talk to her.

He rubbed his hand across the back of his neck. "Could you give me ten minutes?"

"For what?"

He smiled as charmingly as he could, deciding to pretend this was a business conversation so he'd get some of his control back. "Ten minutes, Liz. That's all I want."

Liz sighed and glanced at the woman beside her.

She shrugged. "You could go outside to the patio."

Cain blanched. "This isn't your house?"

"No."

He squeezed his eyes shut in embarrassment, then addressed the redhead. "I'm sorry. Ms.—"

"It's Amanda." She shrugged. "And don't worry about it. It's not really my house, either."

"Then whose house is it?"

Liz motioned for him to follow her down the hall and into the kitchen. "I'll explain on the patio."

The little girl with the big blue eyes also followed them to the sliding glass door. Liz stopped short of exiting, stooping to the toddler's level. "Joy, you stay with your mom, okay?"

Grinning shyly, Joy nodded.

Liz smiled and hugged her fiercely, before she rose. Something odd bubbled up inside Cain, something he'd never once considered while they were married. Liz would make a wonderful mom. He'd known she'd wanted children, but after his brother's death, they'd never again discussed it. Was that why she'd left him without a word? And if it was—if what meant the most to her was having a child—how could he possibly make *that* up to her?

Without looking at him she said, "This way."

She led him to a small stone patio with an inexpensive umbrella-covered table. There was no pool, no outdoor kitchen. Just a tiny gas grill.

She sat at the table and he did the same. "Whose house is this?"

"It's owned by a charity." Lowering her voice to a whisper, she leaned in closer so he could hear her. "Look, Cain, I really can't tell you much, except this house belongs to a charity for women who need a second chance. They stay at houses like this until they can get on their feet."

Cain didn't have to work hard to read between the lines of what she'd said. He frowned. "She's been abused?"

Liz shushed him with a wave of her hand and whispered, "Yes." Lowering her voice even more she added, "Look, we don't like talking about this when we're with the clients. We're trying to establish them as any other member of their community. Not someone being supported by a charity. We want them to think of us as friends, not benefactors."

Following her direction to keep the conversation more private, Cain leaned closer to Liz. The light scent of her shampoo drifted over to him. The smoothness of her skin called him to touch. Memories tripped over themselves in his brain until he remembered this was how she'd been the day he'd met her on the plane. Sweet. Kind. Shy. Reluctant to talk. He'd had to draw her out even to get her to tell him the simplest things about herself.

That day he hadn't been bad at normal conversation. He'd wanted to sleep with her enough that he'd pushed beyond his inability to chitchat.

He rubbed his hand across the back of his neck. That was a bad connection to make with her sitting so close, smelling like heaven, while his own blood vibrated through his veins with recognition that this woman had once been his.

He cleared his throat. "So, this is a charity?"

"Yes." She winced.

He glanced around, confused. "What are *you* doing here?"

"Happy Maids donates housecleaning services when one of the Friend Indeed houses becomes vacant. I also stock the cupboards with groceries and cleaning supplies. I'm part of the committee that welcomes a woman to her new house and stays in her life to help her acclimate."

"A Friend Indeed?"

She nodded.

Processing everything she'd told him, Cain stayed silent. He'd accomplished his purpose. A woman who not only donated the services of her business, but also bought groceries, was obviously committed to this charity. Anything he did for A Friend Indeed would be a kindness to her. Clearly, they'd won her heart. So all he had to do was make a big contribution, and his conscience would be clear.

But figuring that out also meant he had nothing more to say.

He could try to make up a reason to talk to her,

but he'd already proven chitchat wasn't his forte. Plus, that would only mean staying longer with the woman whose mere presence made him ache for what they'd had and lost. There was no point wanting what he couldn't have. They'd been married once. It had failed.

Exhaling a big breath, Cain rose. "I'm sorry I bothered you."

Her brow puckering in confusion, she rose with him. "I thought you wanted to talk."

"We just did." Rather than return to the kitchen and leave through the front door, he glanced around, saw the strip of sidewalk surrounding the house that probably led to the driveway and headed off.

His conscience tweaked again at the fact that he'd confused her but he ignored it. The money he would donate would more than make up for it.

On Monday morning, he had Ava investigate A Friend Indeed. At first she found very little beyond their name and their registration as a charitable organization, then Cain called in a few favors and doors began to open. Though shrouded in secrecy, the charity checked out and on Friday morning Cain had Ava write a check and deliver it to the home of the president of the group's board of directors. She returned a few hours later chuckling.

"Ayleen Francis wants to meet you."

Cain glanced up from the document he was reading. "Meet me?"

She leaned against the door frame. "I did the usual spiel that I do when you have me deliver a check like this. That you admire the work being done by the group and want to help, but prefer to remain anonymous, et cetera. And she said that was fine but she wouldn't accept your check unless she met you."

Cain frowned. "Seriously?"

"That's what she said."

"But—" Damn it. Why did everything about Liz have to turn complicated? "Why would she want to meet me?"

"To thank you?"

Annoyed, he growled. "I don't need thanks."

Ava shrugged. "I have no idea what's going on. I'm just the messenger." She set the check and a business card on Cain's desk. "Here's the address. She said it would be wonderful if you could be there tonight at eight."

Cain snatched up the card and damned near threw it in the trash. But he stopped. He was *this* close to making it up to Liz for their marriage being a disaster. No matter how much he'd worked with his dad before he sold the family business in Kansas and retired, Cain had never been able to do enough to make up for his brother's death. His parents had accepted Tom's death as an accident and eventually Cain had, too. Sort of. As the driver of the car, he would always feel responsible. He'd never let go of that guilt. But he did understand it had been an accident.

But his troubled marriage wasn't an accident. He'd coerced Liz. Seduced her. More sexually experienced than she had been, he'd taken advantage of their chemistry. Used it. She hadn't stood a chance.

And he knew he had to make that up to her. Was he really going to let one oddball request stand in his way of finally feeling freed of the debt?

CHAPTER FOUR

ARRANGING HER NOTES for the executive board meeting for A Friend Indeed held the first Friday of the month, Liz sat at the long table in the conference room of the accounting firm that handled the finances for the charity. The firm also lent them space to hold their meetings because A Friend Indeed didn't want to waste money on an office that wouldn't often be used. Their work was in the field.

Ayleen Francis, a fiftysomething socialite with blond hair and a ready smile who was the president of the board, sat at the head of the table chatting with Ronald Johnson, a local man whose daughter had been murdered by an ex-boyfriend. A Friend Indeed had actually been Ron's brainchild, but it took Ayleen's money and clout to bring his dream to fruition.

Beside Ron was Rose Swartz, owner of a chain of floral shops. Liberty Myers sat next to Rose and beside Liz was Bill Brown. The actual board for the group consisted of sixteen members, but the six-person executive board handled most of the day-to-day decisions.

Waiting for Ayleen to begin the meeting, Liz handed the receipts for the groceries she'd purchased for Amanda and her kids to Rose, the group's treasurer, as well as a statement for cleaning services. Liz donated both the food and the services, but for accounting purposes A Friend Indeed kept track of what each cost.

"Thank you, Liz," Rose said, her smile warm and appreciative. But before Liz could say you're welcome, someone entered behind her and a hush fell over the small group.

Ayleen rose just as Liz turned to see Cain standing in the door way. "I'm assuming you're Cain Nestor."

He nodded.

Ayleen smiled and turned to the group. "Every-

one, this is Cain Nestor, CEO of Cain Corporation. He's visiting us this evening."

Shock and confusion rippled through Liz. She
hadn't seen Cain in three years, now suddenly he
was everywhere! Worse, she'd brought him here.
She'd given him the name of the group when he
followed her to Amanda's. She couldn't believe
he was still pursuing the opportunity to thank
her for staying with him while he was sick, but
apparently he was and she didn't like it. She was
over him. She wanted to stay over him!

"Just take a seat anywhere." Ayleen motioned
to the empty seats at the end of the table.

Cain didn't move from the doorway. "Ms. Francis—"

Ayleen smiled sweetly. "Call me Ayleen."

"Ayleen, could we talk privately?"

"Actually, I don't say or do much for A Friend
Indeed without my executive board present.
That's why I asked your assistant to pass on the
message for you to meet me here. If you'll let me
start the meeting, I'll tell the group about your
donation—"

Liz frowned. He'd made a donation? To *her* charity?

"My assistant was also supposed to tell you that the donation was to be kept confidential."

"Everything about A Friend Indeed is confidential." She motioned around the room. "Nothing about the group goes beyond the board of directors. Some things don't go beyond the six people at this table. However, none of us keeps secrets from the others. But if you don't care to stay for the meeting, then I'll simply tell the group I'm refusing your donation."

Cain gaped at her. "What?"

"Mr. Nestor, though we appreciate your money, what we really need is your help." She ambled to the conference-room door. "As I've already mentioned, everything about A Friend Indeed is confidential. That's out of necessity. We give women a place to stay after they leave abusive husbands or boyfriends." She smiled engagingly as she slid her arm beneath Cain's and guided him into the room.

"For their safety, we promise complete anonymity. But because we do promise complete anonymity to our clients, we can't simply hire construction firms to come and do repair work on our houses. As a result, several of them are in serious disrepair."

Liz sat up, suddenly understanding the point Ayleen was about to make. The group didn't need money as much as they needed skilled, trustworthy volunteers.

"The amount of your check is wonderful. But what we really need is help. If you seriously want to do something for this group, what we'd like is your time."

Cain glanced at Liz, then returned his gaze to Ayleen. "What are you saying?"

"I'm asking you to do some work for us."

He looked at Liz again. Her skin heated. Her heartbeat jumped to double-time. He was actually considering it.

For her.

Something warm and syrupy flooded her system. He'd never done anything like this. It was overkill as a thank-you for her helping him through the flu. Donating money was more within his comfort zone. Especially donating anonymously. A secret donation of money, no matter how big, was easy for him.

But A Friend Indeed didn't need his money as much as his help. And he was considering it.

Holding his gaze, Liz saw the debate in his eyes. He'd have to give up time, work with people. Ordinary people. Because someone from A Friend Indeed would have to accompany him. A stranger couldn't go to the home of one of their abused women alone.

But, his money hadn't been accepted. If he still wanted to do something nice for Liz, it would require his time. Something he rarely gave.

Continuing to hold Liz's gaze he said, "What would I have to do?"

Liz smiled. Slowly. Gratefully. She didn't care as much about a thank-you as she cared about A Friend Indeed. About the families in the homes that needed repairs. She'd been up close and personal with most of them, since her group was in charge of cleaning them for the families, and she knew just how bad some of the homes were.

Alyeen said, "Liz? What would he have to do?"

Liz faced Ayleen. "Cain paid his way through university working construction jobs in the summer. If he could spare the time, the house we moved Amanda into a few weeks ago has a lot of little things that need to be repaired."

"It's been years since I've done any hands-on construction. I can't make any promises without seeing the house."

Ayleen clapped her hands together with glee. "Understandable. I'll have Liz take you to Amanda's."

Liz's heart thumped. She wanted his help, the group *needed* his help, but she didn't want to have to be with him to get it.

"I'm not sure I can," Liz said at the same time that Cain said, "That's not necessary."

"You're a stranger to us," Ayleen firmly told Cain. "For the safety and assurance of our families, I want you with someone from the board at all times." She faced Liz. "Liz, you've been at Amanda's every weekend since she moved in anyway. And you obviously know Cain. You're the best person to accompany him to Amanda's tomorrow." She smiled at Liz. "Please."

Drat. She shouldn't have mentioned her knowledge about Cain's construction experience. But she had been amazed and grateful that he was willing to help. She'd be crazy or shrewish to refuse to do her part.

"Sure."

Ayleen maneuvered Cain into a seat, but not once did Liz even glance in his direction. It was one thing to appreciate the gift of his help, quite another to be stuck spending time with him. Worse, the whole idea that he'd be willing to actually work, *physically work*, to thank her for a few hours of caring for him gave her a soft fluttery feeling in her stomach.

She ignored it. They had to spend time together the next day. Maybe hours. She couldn't be all soft and happy—but she couldn't be angry with him, either. He was doing a huge favor for a charity that meant a great deal to her.

Of course he'd wanted to do it anonymously. Being with her probably wasn't a happy prospect for him any more than it was for her. With anybody else she'd be figuring out a way to make this deal palatable for them. So maybe that's what she needed to do with Cain. Find a way to make this easy for him, as if they were two friends working together for a charity.

The thought caused her brow to furrow. They'd never been friends. They'd been passionate lovers. A distant married couple. Hurt divorced people. But they'd never really been friends. They'd never even tried to be friends.

Maybe becoming friends was the real way for them to get beyond their troubled marriage? To pretend, even if only for a few hours, that the past was the past and from this point on they were two nice people trying to help each other.

Cain was already at Amanda's house the next morning when Liz arrived. Instead of his black Porsche, he waited for her in one of his Nestor Construction trucks. An old red one.

Keeping with her decision to treat him as she would a friend, she smiled and patted the side of the truck bed. "Wow. I haven't seen one of these in years."

He walked around the truck and Liz's smile disappeared as her mouth fell open slightly. She'd already noticed his T-shirt, but for some reason or another, the jeans he wore caught her off guard. He looked so young. So capable. So…sexy.

She cleared her throat, reminding herself that this was a new era for her and Cain. Friends. Two nice people working together for a charity.

"Mostly, we use Cain Corporation trucks now." He grinned. "But when I ran Nestor Construction, this one was mine." He patted the wheel well. "She was my first."

"Ah, a man and his truck." Eager to get out of the sun and to the reason they were here, Liz turned to the sidewalk. "Come on. This way."

They walked to the front door and Liz knocked. Joy answered, but Amanda was only a few feet behind her. She grabbed the giggling three-year-old and hoisted her into her arms. "Sorry about that."

Liz laughed. "Good morning, Joy," she said, tweaking the little girl's cheek as she passed.

Joy buried her face in Amanda's neck. "Morning."

Amanda looked pointedly at Cain. "And this is Cain?"

Cain held out his hand for shaking. "Sorry about our first meeting."

Amanda smiled. "That's okay. Neither one of us was in good form that day. Can I get you some coffee?"

Cain peered over at Liz.

Liz motioned for everyone to go into the kitchen. "Of course, we'd love some coffee."

When Amanda walked through the swinging door out of sight, Liz caught Cain's arm, holding him back. "If she offers something, take it. A lot of the women who come to us have little to no self-esteem. It makes them feel good about themselves to have coffee or doughnuts to offer. Take whatever she offers and eat it."

Looking sheepish and unsure, he nodded and everything inside Liz stilled. For the first time in their relationship she knew something he didn't. He needed her.

Their gazes caught.

Liz smiled, downplaying the reversal of their roles and seeking to reassure him.

The corners of his mouth edged up slowly in response, and his entire countenance changed. Crinkles formed around dark eyes that warmed.

The hallway suddenly felt small and quiet. The memory of how much she'd loved this man fluttered through her. With one step forward she could lay her palm on his cheek. Touch him. Feel his skin again. Feel connected to him in the only way they'd ever been connected. Touch.

But one touch always led to another and another and another. Which was probably why making love was the only way they'd bonded. They'd never had a chance to be friends. Never given themselves a chance to get to know each other.

Sad, really.

Instead of stepping forward, she stepped back, motioning to the door. "After you."

He shook his head. His voice was rich, husky when he said, "No. After you."

He'd been as affected by the moment as she had been. For a second she couldn't move, couldn't breathe, as another possibility for why he'd been so insistent on thanking her popped into her head. He hadn't forgotten their sexual chemistry any more than she had. They hadn't been good as a married couple, but they had been fantastic lovers. What if he was being kind, using this "thankyou" as a first step to seducing her?

A sickening feeling rose up in her. He hadn't hesitated the first time. He'd done everything he'd had to do to get her to Miami, into his bed. Working for a charity was small potatoes compared to some of the things he'd done to woo her, including whisk her to Vegas and seduce her into marrying him.

Well, six years later she wasn't so foolish. So young. So inexperienced. If he dared as much as make a pass at her, he'd find himself with a new Friend Indeed employee as his liaison. He'd still have to fulfill his end of the bargain. He just wouldn't do it with her.

She headed for the swinging door. Cain followed. In the kitchen, Amanda already had three mugs of coffee on the table. The room was spotless and smelled of maple syrup. Amanda had the look of a woman who'd happily served her daughter breakfast.

Cain took a seat at the table. "We can use this time to talk about what you need me to do."

"You're doing the work?"

Liz caught Amanda's hand, forcing her gaze to hers for reassurance. "Yes. Cain worked in construction to put himself through university."

"And as a bartender and a grocery boy. I was also a waiter and amusement-park vendor." He smiled at Amanda as she sat. "School was four long years."

Amanda laughed.

Liz pulled her hand away. "So go ahead. Give Cain the list of things that need to be done."

"First, the plumbing."

He took a small notebook from his shirt pocket. "Okay."

"There are some places with missing baseboard."

"Uh-huh."

"The ceiling in the first bedroom has water marks."

Without looking up from his note taking, Cain said, "That's not good."

"And most of the walls need to be painted."

"You guys can help with that."

Liz hesitated. She didn't want to agree to time in the same room with him, but from the sounds of the list Cain's work here wouldn't be a few hours. He'd be here for days and Liz would be, too. If she had to be here to oversee things, she might as well have something to do. Plus, the more she did, the sooner her time with Cain would be over.

"Sure."

Because Amanda had stopped listing repair items, Cain finally glanced up. "That's it?"

"Isn't that enough?"

"It's plenty. In fact," he said with a wince, "if those water marks are roof leaks, we've got a problem."

"Why?"

Cain caught Liz's gaze and her insides turned to gelatin again. But not because of chemistry. Because of fear. His eyes were soft, his expression grave. He wanted to do a good job. But he also had to be honest.

She'd only seen him look this way once. When she'd told him she couldn't plan a huge Christmas party he'd wanted to host for his business associates. She'd been afraid—terrified really—that she'd do something wrong, something simple, but so awful that she'd embarrass them both. He'd been angry first, but that emotion had flitted from his face quickly and was replaced by the expression he now wore. It had disappointed him that she couldn't do what he needed, but he had to be honest and admit he still wanted the party. So he'd hired someone to plan it for him.

He'd moved beyond it as if it wasn't a big

deal. But the disappointment he'd felt in her lingered. Even now it reminded her that he knew they weren't good for each other as a couple. They didn't match. He wouldn't want to start something with her any more than she'd want to start something with him. No matter how sexually compatible they were, he wasn't here to seduce her. She actually felt a little foolish for even thinking it.

"A roof isn't a one-man job. Even with a crew a roof takes a few days. At the very least a weekend." He looked at Amanda. "But I'll choose the crew with care."

Amanda looked at Liz.

"We'll talk it over with Ayleen, but we can trust Cain. If he says he'll figure out a way to keep all this confidential, he'll do it." When it came to work Cain was as good as his word. "Plus, if Cain's okay with it, we'll only work weekends and you can take the kids to the beach or something. Not be around. Just to be sure no one sees you."

Amanda nodded. "Okay."

"Okay." Cain rose. "Let me take a quick look at all these things then I'll make a trip to the building supply store."

"Toilets are fixed. Showers all work," Cain said, wiping his hands on a paper towel as he walked into the kitchen.

Amanda had made grilled cheese sandwiches and tomato soup for lunch. Liz already sat at the table. Amanda was happily serving. He took a seat and Liz smiled at him. After walking through the house with him behaving like a contractor, not her ex-husband, not the man she shared unbelievable chemistry with, Liz was slightly annoyed with herself for even considering he was only here as part of a plan to seduce her. His work here might have begun as a way to thank her for caring for him, but now that he was here, he clearly wanted to do a good job. It almost seemed he'd forgotten their chemistry or that she had imagined his reaction as they stood in the hallway that morning.

Which was good. Excellent. And took her back to her plan of behaving like his friend.

"So this afternoon we paint?"

"I'd like to get the painting done before we put up new baseboards. With all the rooms that need to be painted, it's going to take a few days. So it would be best if we started immediately after we eat."

"Okay."

Liz took a sandwich from the platter Amanda passed to her and handed it to Cain. Things were good. Relaxed. The more she was in his company this way, the more confident and comfortable she felt around him.

"I'll do the ceilings," Cain said, taking three sandwiches. "You guys handle the walls."

Amanda grimaced. "I'm sorry. I scheduled a playdate for Joy. I didn't realize you'd need me this soon."

"It's all right," Liz said easily. "Cain and I will be fine."

She genuinely believed that, until Amanda and Joy left and suddenly she and Cain were alone with two gallons of paint, two paint trays and a few brushes and rollers. Why did fate always have to test her like this? Just because she'd become comfortable around him, that didn't mean she had to be tested an hour after the thought had formed in her brain.

"What's the protocol on this?" she asked, nervously flitting away from him.

"First, we put blue tape around the windows and doors and existing baseboards so we don't get any paint where we don't want it. Then I'll do the ceiling and you do the walls."

He went out to his truck and returned with a roll of blue tape. Swiftly, without a second thought and as if he weren't having any trouble being alone with her, he applied it on the wood trim around the windows.

"Wow. A person would never guess you hadn't done that in about ten years."

He laughed. "It's like riding a bike. It comes back to you."

He *was* at ease. He wasn't seeing her as anything but a work buddy. Surely, she could follow suit.

"I know but you really look like you were born to this. It's almost a shame you don't do it anymore."

"My end of things is equally important." He turned from the window. "Come here. Let me show you how simple it is."

She walked over to the window and he positioned her in front of it. Handing her the roll, he said, "Hook the end of the tape over the edge of the top molding and then just roll it down."

She did as he said but the tape angled inward and by the time she reached the bottom the edge was still bare.

"Here." Covering her hand with his, he showed her how to direct the roll as she moved it downward, so that the side of the woodwork was entirely covered by the tape.

Liz barely noticed. With his chest brushing her back and his arm sliding along her arm, old feelings burst inside her. The scent of him drifted to her and she squeezed her eyes shut. She had never met a man who caused such a riot inside her. She longed to turn around and snuggle into him, wrap her arms around him, simply enjoy the feeling of his big body against hers.

She stiffened. She had to get beyond this! If he could treat her like a coworker, she could treat him like a friend.

As if unfazed, he pulled away and walked to the paint. He poured some of the gray into one of the trays and white into the second one.

"Okay. I'm ceilings. You're walls. But first I'm going to do the edge where the wall meets the ceiling." He nodded at the tray of gray paint. "You take that and a roller and go nuts on the walls. Just stay away from the edges."

"With pleasure." She managed to make her voice sound light and friendly, but inside she was a mess. Especially since he seemed so cavalier. All this time she'd believed his attraction to her fueled her attraction to him. Now, she wasn't so sure. Oh, she still believed he was attracted to her. His attraction simply didn't control him.

And by God she wasn't going to let hers control her, either!

For the next ten minutes they were quiet. Cain took a brush and painted an incredibly straight, incredibly neat six-inch swatch at the top of the wall, ensuring that Liz wouldn't even accidentally get any gray paint on the ceiling.

Deciding she needed to bring them back to a neutral place or the silence would make her nuts by the end of the day she said, "How do you do that so fast, yet so well?"

"Lots and lots of practice," he said, preoccupied with pouring more white paint into his tray. "Don't forget I did this kind of work four summers in a row. That was how I knew I wanted to run a construction company. I learned to do just about everything and I actually knew the work involved when I read plans or specs."

"Makes sense." She rolled gray paint onto the far wall. She'd heard that story before, but now that she was a business owner she understood it and could respond to it.

"In a way, I got into cleaning for the same reason. Once I realized what would be required of my employees, it was easy to know who to choose for what jobs and also what to charge."

"And you did great."

His praise brought a lump to her throat. In the three years they were married he'd never praised her beyond her looks. He loved how she looked, how she smelled, how soft she was. But he'd never noticed her beyond that.

She cleared her throat. "Thanks."

Occupied with painting the ceiling, Cain quietly said, "You know this is going to be more than a one-day job."

"So you've said."

He winced. "More than a two-week job."

She stopped. "Really?"

"Because we can only work weekends, I'm thinking we're in this for a month. And we're kind of going to be stuck together."

"Are you bailing?"

"No!" His answer was sharp. He stopped painting and faced her. "No. But I have to warn you that I'm a little confused about how to treat you."

Relief stuttered through her. She didn't want him to seduce her, but she certainly didn't want to be the only one fighting an attraction. "I thought we were trying to behave like friends."

"I'm not sure how to do that."

"Most of the day you've been treating me like a coworker. Why don't you go back to that? Forget I'm your ex-wife."

He glanced over at her and all the air evaporated from Liz's lungs. The look he gave her was long and slow, as if asking how he could forget that they'd been married, been intimate.

Maybe that was the crux of their problem? Every time she looked at him something inside her stirred to life. She'd lived for three years without thinking about sex, but put him in the room with her and she needed to fan herself. Worse, through nearly three years of a bad marriage, they'd already proven they could be angry with each other, all wrong for each other and still pleasure each other beyond belief.

It was going to be difficult to pretend none of that mattered.

But they had to try.

She cleared her throat. "I could use a glass of water. Would you like one?"

"Please."

In the kitchen, she took two bottles of water from the refrigerator. She pressed the cool container against her cheek. Late March in southern Florida could be hot, but being in the same room with Cain was turning out to be even hotter.

Still, A Friend Indeed needed his help. Amanda deserved a pretty home for herself and her kids. Liz was also a strong, determined business-woman who had handled some fairly tough trials through the three years of running her company. One little attraction wasn't going to ruin her.

Feeling better, she walked back to the living room, but stopped dead in the doorway. Reaching up to paint the ceiling, with his back to her, Cain stretched his T-shirt taut against his muscles. His jeans snugly outlined his behind. She swallowed. Memories of them in the shower and tangled in their sheets flashed through her brain.

She pressed the water bottle to her cheek again,

pushing the pointless memories aside, and strode up behind him.

"Here."

He turned abruptly and a few drops of paint rained on her nose.

"Oops! Sorry. You kind of surprised me."

"It's okay."

He yanked a work hanky from his back pocket. "Let me get that."

Enclosing her chin in his big hand to hold her head still, he rubbed the cloth against her nose. Memories returned full force. Times he'd kissed her. Laughing on the beach before running into the house for mind-blowing sex. Falling asleep spooned together after.

He blinked. His hand stilled. Everything she was feeling was reflected in his dark eyes.

The world stopped for Liz. Holding his gaze, knowing exactly what he was remembering, feeling the thrum of her own heart as a result of the memories that poured through her brain, Liz couldn't move, couldn't breathe.

For ten seconds she was absolutely positive he

was going to kiss her. The urge to stand on her tiptoes and accept a kiss was so strong she had to fight it with everything in her. But in the end, he backed away, his hand falling to his side.

Turning to the wall again, he said, "Another twenty minutes and I'll have the ceiling done. If you want to go put blue tape around the windows in the dining room we could probably get that room done today, too."

She stepped back. "Okay." She took another step backward toward the door. "Don't forget your water."

He didn't look up. "I won't."

Relief rattled through her. He'd just had a golden opportunity to kiss her, yet he'd stepped away.

She definitely wasn't the only one who wanted them to be friends, not lovers, or the only one who'd changed.

When Liz was gone, Cain lowered himself to the floor. Leaning against the old stone fireplace, he rubbed his hand down his face.

He could have kissed her. Not out of habit. Not out of instinct driven by happy memories. But because he wanted to. He *longed* to. She'd hardly left the house for their entire marriage. Now she was a business owner, a volunteer for a charity, a confident, self-sufficient woman. This new side of Liz he was seeing was very appealing. When he coupled her new personality with his blissful sexual memories, she was damned near irresistible.

But the clincher—the thing that almost took him over the top—was the way she looked at him as if she'd never stopped loving him. As if she wanted what he wanted. As if her entire body revved with anticipation, the way his did. As if her heart was open and begging.

He'd always known he was the problem in their marriage. And now that he was older and wiser, he desperately wanted to fix things. But he didn't want to hurt her again. He saw the trust in her eyes. Sweet, innocent trust. She was counting on him to do the right thing.

Part of him genuinely believed the right thing

was to leave her alone. Let her get on with her life. Become the success she was destined to be.

The other part just kept thinking that she was his woman, and he wanted her back.

But he knew that was impossible.

CHAPTER FIVE

WHILE THEY WORKED, Amanda and Joy returned from Joy's playdate, and Amanda prepared a barbecue. Liz didn't realize she was cooking until the aroma of tangy barbeque sauce floated through the downstairs. Just the scent brought Liz to the patio. A minute later, Cain followed behind her.

"What is that smell?"

Amanda laughed. "It's my mother's special barbeque-sauce recipe. Have a seat. Everything's done."

A glance to the right showed the umbrella table had been set with paper plates and plastic utensils. A bowl of potato salad sat beside some baked beans and a basket of rolls.

Starving from all the work she'd done, Liz sat down without a second thought. Cain, however, debated. She couldn't imagine how a single man could turn down home cooking until she remembered their near miss with the kiss. Their gazes caught. He looked away.

She could guess what he was thinking. It was getting harder and harder to work together because the longer they were together the more tempted they were. But his stepping away from the kiss proved he was here to help, only to help, not to try to work his way back into her bed.

And that meant she was safe. But so was he. He simply didn't know that she was as determined as he was to get beyond their attraction. Perhaps even to be friends.

So maybe she had to show him?

"Come on, Cain. This smells too good to resist."

He caught her gaze and she smiled encouragingly. She tried to show him with her expression that everything was okay. They could be around each other, if he'd just relax.

He walked to the table. "You're right. Especially since I'd be going home to takeout."

He sat across the table from her, leaving the two seats on either side of her for Amanda and Joy.

She smiled. As long as they paid no attention to their attraction, they could work toward becoming friends. She would simply have to ignore the extreme sadness that welled in her heart, now that their glances would no longer be heated and they had both silently stated their intentions not to get involved again. Mourning something that hadn't worked was ridiculous. She didn't want to go back to what they had. Apparently neither did he. So at least trying to become friends would make the next few weeks easier.

"Where's Billy?"

"Beach with some friends," Amanda announced casually. Then she paused and grinned. "You can't believe how wonderful it feels to say that. We were always so worried about Rick's reaction to everything that most of the time we didn't talk. Telling him where Billy was was an invitation to get into an argument." She shook her head. "It was no way to live."

"No. It isn't."

That came from Cain and caused Liz's head to swivel in his direction. Not only was he not one to talk about such personal things, but his sympathetic tone was so unexpected she almost couldn't believe it was he who had spoken.

"Men who abuse anyone weaker than they are are scum." His voice gentled and he glanced at Amanda. "I'm glad you're safe."

Liz stared at him, suddenly understanding. He'd never been a bad person, simply an overly busy person who had never stopped long enough to pay attention to anything that didn't pop up in front of him. Amanda and her children were no longer an "issue" to him. They were people with names and faces and lives. It lightened Liz's heart that he didn't just recognize that; he genuinely seemed to care for them.

Still, the conversation could potentially dip into subjects too serious for Joy's ears. "Well, that's all over now," Liz said, turning to the little girl. "And how did you like your playdate?"

Joy leaned across the table. "It was fun. Maddie has a cat."

"A huge monster cat!" Amanda said, picking up the platter of chicken and spearing a barbecued breast. "I swear I thought it was a dog when I first saw it."

They laughed.

"Do you have a cat?" Joy asked Liz.

"No. No cat for me. I'm allergic."

"It means she can't be around them or she'll sneeze," Amanda explained to Joy as she passed the beans to Cain.

"I didn't know you were allergic to cats."

That was Cain. His words were soft, not sharp or accusatory, but trepidation rippled through her, reminding her of another reason she and Cain couldn't be more than coworkers. She had bigger secrets than an allergy to cats. From the day she'd met him she'd kept her father's abuse a secret. Plus, she'd never told him they'd created a child, and then she'd lost that child.

If they weren't with Amanda, this might have been the time to tell him. They'd had a reasonably pleasant afternoon. They'd both silently stated their intention not to get involved, but to try to be friends. That had created a kind of bond of honesty between them, which would have made this the perfect time to at least tell him about his child.

But they weren't alone.

Liz turned her attention to the platter of chicken that had come her way. "You didn't have a cat. I didn't have a cat. It never came up."

He accepted her answer easily, but shame buffeted her, an unexpected result of spending so much time in his company. With him behaving like a good guy, a normal guy, a guy who wanted to get beyond their sexual chemistry and be friends, the secrets she'd kept in their marriage suddenly seemed incredibly wrong.

She hadn't told him that her dad had abused her, her mom and her sisters because at the time she was working to forget that. To build a life without her other life hanging over her head. She hadn't told him about her miscarriage because she'd needed help herself to accept it. And she'd had to leave him to get that help.

But three years later, so far beyond both of

those problems that she could speak about each without breaking down, she wondered about the wisdom of having kept her secrets from him.

Would their marriage have been different if she'd admitted that as a child she'd been poor, hungry and constantly afraid?

Would *he* have been different if she'd turned to him for comfort in her time of need?

She'd never know the answer to, either, but the possibility that she could have changed her marriage, saved it, with a few whispered words, haunted her.

Sitting at the kitchen table of Amanda's house the next morning, finishing a cup of coffee after eating delicious blueberry pancakes, Liz smiled shakily at Cain as he stepped into the room. "Good morning."

"Good morning."

She might have kept secrets but she and Cain were now divorced, trying to get along while they worked together, not trying to reconcile. For that reason, she'd decided that the story of her abusive father could remain her secret. But as she had paced the floor the night before, working all this out in her brain, she realized how much she wanted to tell him about their baby.

When they divorced, she had been too raw and too hurt herself to tell him. By the time she'd gotten herself together, their paths never crossed. But now that their paths hadn't merely crossed, they were actually intersecting for the next several weeks; she couldn't keep the secret from him any more. He'd created a child. They'd lost that child. He deserved to know. And she wanted to tell him.

Which left her with two problems. When she'd tell him and how she'd tell him. She might be ready to share, but he might not be ready to hear it. She had to be alert for another opportunity like the one the day before…except when they were alone, not with other people.

Amanda turned from the stove. "Are you hungry, Cain? I'm making blueberry pancakes."

It was clear that Amanda reveled in the role of mom. Without the constant fear of her abusive husband she had blossomed. Joy was bright-eyed and happy, a little chatterbox who had entertained Liz all through breakfast. Amanda's only remaining problem was Billy, her sixteen-year-old son. They hadn't been away from their violent father long enough for any one of them to have adjusted, but once they had, Liz was certain Amanda would think of some way to connect with her son.

As far as Amanda's situation was concerned, Liz could relax…except for Cain, who hesitated just inside the kitchen door. Had he figured out she'd kept secrets bigger than an allergy to cats? Was he angry? Would he confront her? She couldn't handle that. Telling him about their baby had to be on her terms. That would be better for both of them. It would be horrible if he confronted her now.

Finally he said, "I've already eaten breakfast."

Relief wanted to rush out of her on a long gust of air, but she held it back. She'd instructed him to take everything Amanda offered. The day before he could have easily begged off her barbecue by saying it was time to go home. But he couldn't so easily walk away from breakfast when he would be staying all morning.

Amanda said, "That's okay. Just have some coffee." She reached for a mug from the cupboard by the stove, filled it and handed it to him. "Sit for a minute."

He took the coffee and he and Amanda ambled to chairs at the table, as Amanda's sixteen-year-old son Billy stepped into the room, music headphones in his ears. Totally oblivious to the people at the table, he walked to the refrigerator and pulled out the milk.

Amanda cast an embarrassed glance at her son. "Billy, at least say good-morning."

He ignored her.

She rose, walked over to him and took one of the headphones from his right ear. "Good morning," she singsonged.

Billy sighed. "Morning."

"Say good morning to our guests."

He scowled toward the table. "Good morning."

Liz had seen this a million times before. A

teenager embarrassed that he had to count on a charity for a roof over his head frequently acted out. Especially the son of an abusive father. Even as Billy was probably glad to get away from his dad, he also missed him. Worse, he could be wondering about himself. If he was like his dad.

Liz's gaze slid to Cain. Billy was the kind of employee Cain hated. Troubled. He wanted only the best, both emotionally and physically, so he didn't have to deal with problems. His job was to get whatever construction project he had done and done right. He didn't have time for employee problems.

But after the way he'd reacted to Amanda's comment the day before, Liz knew he'd changed. At least somewhat. And he did have a soft spot for Amanda and her family. Billy was a part of that family. He desperately needed a positive male role model. If Cain simply behaved as he had the day before when he showed her how to use the blue tape and paint, Billy might actually learn something.

Plus, she and Cain wouldn't have to be in the same room.

She didn't want to spend the day worrying about how and when she'd tell him about their child. She also couldn't simply blurt it out in an awkward silence, particularly since they might be alone in the room but they weren't alone in the house. She wanted the right opportunity again, but she also needed time to think it through so she could choose her words carefully. Not being around Cain would buy her time.

She took a breath then smiled at Billy. "We could sure use your help today. Especially Cain."

Amanda gasped and clasped her hands together. "What a wonderful idea! Do you know who Mr. Nestor is?"

Billy rolled his eyes. "No."

"He owns a construction company." Amanda all but glowed with enthusiasm. "I'll bet he could teach you a million things."

"I don't need to know a million things, Mom. Besides, I want to go to med school."

"And you're going to need money," Amanda

pointed out. "Mr. Nestor put himself through university working construction."

Billy glared at Cain.

Cain shifted uncomfortably. "Construction isn't for everyone," he said, clearly unhappy to be caught in the middle. "I was also a bartender."

"But you're here now," Liz said, unable to stop herself. Her gaze roamed over to Cain's. "And you could teach him so much."

She let her eyes say the words she couldn't utter in front of the angry teen who desperately needed to at least see how a decent man behaved.

Cain pulled in a slow breath. Liz held hers. He'd changed. She knew he'd changed just from the sympathy he'd displayed to Amanda the day before. He could do this! All he had to do was say okay.

She held her breath as she held his gaze. His steely eyes bore into hers, but the longer their connection, the more his eyes softened.

Finally, he turned on his chair, facing Billy. "What I'm doing today isn't hard. So it might be a good place for you to start if you're interested in learning a few things."

"There! See!" Amanda clasped Billy on the shoulder. "It will be good for you."

Cain rose and motioned for Billy to follow him out of the kitchen. Liz stared after them, her heart pounding. No matter how much she wanted to believe he'd done that out of sympathy for Amanda's situation, she knew he'd done it for her.

She turned back to her coffee, smiled at Amanda, trying to appear as if nothing was wrong. But everything was wrong. First, spending time with him had caused her to realize he deserved to know he'd created and lost a child. Now he was softening, doing things she asked.

For the first time it occurred to her that maybe he wasn't changing because of their situation but to please her.

And if he was... Lord help them.

Ten minutes later Cain found himself in the living room with an angry, sullen teenager. He debated drawing him into conversation, but somehow he didn't think the charisma that typically worked on egotistical bankers and clever business owners would work with a kid. And the chitchat he was forcing himself to develop with Amanda and Liz hadn't served him all that well, either. He and Billy could either work in silence, or he could hit this kid with the truth.

"You know what? I don't like this any more than you do."

Surprised, Billy looked over.

"But your mom wants you here and every once in a while a man has to suck it up and do what his mom wants." Technically, he and Billy were in the same boat. He was in this room, with this angry boy, because he hadn't been able to resist the pleading in Liz's eyes. And that troubled him. He was falling for her again. Only this time it was different. This time he had nothing to prove professionally. No reason to back away. No way to erect walls that would allow him to be in a relationship and still protect his heart. She'd broken it once. She could do it again.

"If you'd kept your mouth shut I could have gotten out of this."

"How? By being a brat? That's a skill that'll really help you in the real world."

"I don't care about the real world."

Cain snorted. "No kidding." He slid his tape measure from his tool belt and walked to the wall. Holding the end of the tape against the wall, he waved the tape measure's silver container at Billy. "Take this to the other end of the wall."

Billy sighed, but took the tape box and did as Cain requested.

"What's the length?"

"Ten feet."

"Exactly ten feet?"

"I don't know."

Exasperated, but not about to let Billy know that and give him leverage to be a pain all day, Cain said, "Okay. Let's try this again. You hold this end against the wall. I'll get the number."

Without a word, Billy walked the tape back to Cain and they switched places.

He measured the length, told Billy to let go of

his end and the tape snapped back into the silver container. He reached for one of the long pieces of trim he'd purchased the day before. It bowed when he lifted it and he motioned with his chin for Billy to grab the other end. "Get that, will you?"

Billy made a face, but picked up the wood.

Cain carried it to the miter box. The tools he had in his truck were from nearly ten years before. Though they weren't the latest technology they still worked. And maybe teaching this kid a little something today might be the best way to get his mind off Liz. About the fact that he didn't just want her, he was doing crazy things for her. About the fact that if he didn't watch himself, he'd be in so far that he'd be vulnerable again.

"You know, eventually you'll have to go to somebody for a job. You're not going to get through school on your good looks."

Adjusting the wood in the box, Cain made his end cuts. He gestured for Billy to help him take the piece of trim to the wall again. He snapped it into place and secured it with a few shots from a nail gun.

"I was thinking maybe I'd try the bartending thing like you did."

Surprised, Cain glanced over. He cautiously said, "Bartending is good when classes are in session and working nights fits into your schedule. But summers were when I made my tuition. To earn that much money, you have to have a job that pays. Construction pays."

Billy opened his mouth to say something, but snapped it shut. Cain unexpectedly itched to encourage him to talk, but he stopped himself. If the kid wanted to talk, he'd talk. Cain had no intention of overstepping his boundaries. He knew that Liz had set Billy up with him to be a good example, but he wasn't a therapist. Hell, he wasn't even much of a talker. He couldn't believe this kid had gotten as much out of him as he had.

"My dad was—is—in construction."

"Ah." No wonder Liz thought this would be such a wonderful arrangement.

"Look, kid, you don't have to be like your dad. You can be anybody, anything, you want." He glanced around the room. "Doing stuff like this," he said, bringing his words down to Billy's level, "gives you a way to test what you're good at while you figure out who you are." He paused then casually said, "You mentioned that you wanted to go to med school."

"It's a pipe dream. No way I'll swing that."

"Not with that attitude."

Billy snorted. "My mom *can't* help."

"Hey, I made my own way. You can, too." Motioning for Billy to pick up the next board, he casually eased them back into conversation. "Besides, it's a good life lesson. The construction jobs I took to pay for tuition pointed me in the direction of what I wanted to do with my life."

Seeing that Billy was really listening, Cain felt edgy. It would be so easy to steer this kid wrong. He wasn't a people person. He didn't know anything about being raised by an abusive father. There were a million different ways he could make a mistake.

"I think I want to be a doctor, but I'm not sure."

"You'll work that out." He motioned for Billy to grab the tape measure again. "Everything doesn't have to be figured out in one day. Take your time. Give yourself a break. Don't think you have to make all your decisions right now."

Oddly, his advice to Billy also relaxed him about Liz. Every decision didn't have to be made in a day. That's what had screwed them up in the first place. They jumped from seat mates in a plane to dating to sleeping together in a matter of days. Melting and doing her bidding just because she turned her pretty green eyes on him was as bad as working to seduce her the first day he'd met her.

Somehow he had to get back to behaving normally around his wife.

Ex-wife.

Maybe the first step to doing that would be to remember falling victim to their sexual attraction hadn't done anything except toss them into an unhappy marriage.

* * *

Just outside the door, Liz leaned against the wall and breathed an enormous sigh of relief. Two minutes after she suggested Billy help Cain she remembered they'd be using power tools—potential weapons—and she nearly panicked. But it appeared as if Billy and Cain had found a way to get along.

She and Amanda began painting the dining room but at eleven-thirty, they stopped to prepare lunch. At twelve they called Cain and Billy to the kitchen table and to her surprise they were chatting about a big project Cain's company had bid on when they walked to the sink to wash their hands.

They came to the table talking about how Cain's job is part math, part hand-holding and part diplomacy and didn't stop except to grab a bite of sandwich between sentences.

Liz smiled at Cain, working to keep their "friendship" going and determined not to worry about her secret until the time to tell him materialized, but Cain quickly glanced away, as if embarrassed.

When they'd finished eating, Billy and Cain went back to their work and Liz and Amanda cleaned the kitchen then resumed painting.

At five, Liz's muscles were pleasantly sore. She did manual labor for a living, but the muscles required for painting were different than those required for washing windows, vacuuming and dusting. Amanda planned to take her kids out to dinner so Cain and Liz had decided to leave to give them time to clean up before going out.

Still, as tired and sore as she was, she couldn't let Cain go without telling him she was proud of him. Billy needed him and he had cracked some barriers that Amanda had admitted she couldn't crack. After his wary expression when he glanced at her at lunch, she had to tell him how much he was needed, how good a job he was doing.

Leaning against the bed of his truck, waiting as he said goodbye to Amanda and Billy, she smiled as he approached.

"I'm not sure if you're embarrassed because

you didn't want to help Billy or embarrassed that you did such a good job."

He tossed a saw into the toolbox in the bed of his truck. "He's a good kid."

"Of course he is. He just spent the first sixteen years of his life with a man who gave him a very bad impression of what a man's supposed to do. You were a good example today."

"Don't toss my hat in the ring for sainthood."

She laughed.

"I'm serious. If Billy had been a truly angry, truly rebellious teen, I would have been so far out of my league I could have done some real damage."

She sobered. He had a very good point. "I know."

He made a move to open his truck door and Liz stepped away. "I'm sorry."

Climbing into the truck, he shook his head. "No need to apologize. Let's just be glad it worked out."

She nodded. He started his truck and backed out of the driveway.

Liz stared after him. She'd expected him to either be angry that she'd set him up or to preen with pride. Instead, he'd sort of acted normally.

She folded her arms across her chest and watched his truck chug out of the neighborhood and an unexpected question tiptoed into her consciousness. Was acting normally his way of showing her they could be friends... Or his way of easing himself back into her life?

After all, he didn't have to be here, repairing Amanda's house. He could have refused when Ayleen asked him.

He also hadn't needed to befriend Billy. Yet, he'd responded to her silent plea and then did a bang-up job.

He also didn't have to interact with her. She was only here as a chaperone of sorts. Now that the work was going smoothly, he could ignore her.

So what was he doing?

CHAPTER SIX

"HAPPY MAIDS. Liz Harper speaking."

"Good morning, Ms. Harper. It's Ava from Cain Corporation. Mr. Nestor asked me to call."

Liz's heart did a somersault in her chest. Something was wrong. There was no reason for Cain to ask Ava to call except to reprimand her or fire her. Or maybe he'd finally found a full-time maid? It wasn't that she begrudged him help, but with Rita working now, bringing her staff up to seven, she needed every assignment she had and more.

"He's having some friends for a small dinner tonight—"

Liz's heart tumbled again and she squeezed her eyes shut. She wasn't fired. He was inviting her to a party! Oh God! He *was* trying to ease her back into his life.

"He's cooking."

Knowing Cain was very good at the grill, Liz wasn't surprised. But she still didn't want to go to a party at his house. Not when she was just about certain he was trying to get them back together.

"So he won't have a caterer to clean up. He's going to need you to send someone tonight after the party to do that. He'll pay extra, of course."

Liz fell into her office chair, her cheeks flaming. So much for being invited to his party. He wanted her to *clean up*. She was his maid. Not a friend. Not a potential lover or date…or even an ex-wife. She was an employee.

He wasn't trying to ease her into his life. He wasn't even trying to show her they could be friends. He wasn't thinking that hard about it because in his mind there was no longer a question.

He didn't want her.

She swallowed again, easing the lump in her throat so she could speak. That was, after all, what she wanted.

"We'll be happy to clean up after the party."

"You'll only need one person."

No longer upset about the call itself, Liz noticed the pinched, tight tone of Ava's voice.

"It's a small party. Mr. Nestor and the partners of his new venture are gathering to have dinner before they sign a contract. He believes everyone will be gone by nine. Let me suggest you arrive around a quarter after nine."

The first time Liz had spoken with Ava, she'd been light, friendly, eager to get some house-cleaning help for her boss. Today's stiff voice and formal tone puzzled Liz.

"A quarter after nine is fine."

She hung up the phone confused. Could Cain have told his assistant that Liz was his ex-wife? But why would he? What difference would it make? He never shared personal information with employees. Why start now?

Placing her fingers on her computer keyboard to begin inputting her workers' hours on a spreadsheet, she frowned. Even if he had told Ava that Liz was his ex-wife, why would that upset his assistant?

And was that why she hadn't received any referrals from Ava?

She'd expected at least one person to call and say they'd been referred. That was how it worked in Liz's business. Maids had to be trusted. A word-of-mouth recommendation worked better than cold advertising. Yet, she'd gotten no recommendation from Cain.

She shook her head, dislodging those thoughts and getting her mind back on work. She didn't want to waste this precious time she had to do her paperwork fuming and speculating. With Rita working, Liz could now spend afternoons in the office and she basked in having evenings off.

She frowned again. She wouldn't have tonight off. She couldn't ask one of her employees to work on such short notice; all of them had children. Evening work meant extra child-care expenses. Besides, Cain's house was back to being her assignment. After he'd been angry that she'd sent someone else after the waffle debacle, she'd taken the job back herself.

She sighed. She'd have to go to his house tonight.

But maybe that was good?

If nothing else, she had her perspective back.
They were divorced, not trying to reconcile, and
she had something to tell him. Alone in his house
tonight, they could be honest with each other.

A mixture of fear and relief poured through
her. Though telling him about the miscarriage
would be difficult, it had to be done. He deserved
to know.

She finished her paperwork around five and
raced home to shower and change to have dinner with Ellie. She didn't mention that she had
to work that night—

Or the odd tone in Ava's voice—

Or her realization that they hadn't gotten *one*
referral from Cain—

Or that this might be the night she told Cain
the secret she'd kept from him.

All of that would put Ellie on edge. Or cause her
to make one of her powerful wishes. Instead, Liz
listened to Ellie chatter about the Happy Maids

employees. From the sparkle in Ellie's amber eyes it was clear she enjoyed being everyone's supervisor. Not in a lord-it-over-her-friends way. But in almost a motherly way. Which made Liz laugh and actually took her mind off Cain. Ellie was twenty-two. Most of the women she now supervised were in their thirties or forties, some even in their fifties. Yet Ellie clucked over them like a mother hen. It was endearing.

Because they talked about work most of the meal, Liz paid for dinner, calling it a business expense, and parted company with Ellie on the sidewalk in front of the restaurant. When she slid behind the steering wheel of her car and saw the clock on the dashboard her mouth fell open. It was nearly nine. No time to go home and change into a Happy Maids uniform.

She glanced down at her simple tank top and jeans. This would do. No matter how messy his house, she couldn't damage a tank top and jeans.

Worry over being late blanked out all of her other concerns about this job until she pulled

into Cain's empty driveway. Ava had been correct. Cain's guests hadn't lingered. But suddenly
she didn't want to see him. She really wasn't
ready with the "right words" to tell them about
their baby. She wasn't in the mood to "play"
friends, either, or to fight their attraction. Their
marriage might be over, but the attraction hadn't
gone. And that's what made their situation so
difficult.

If they weren't so attracted to each other there
would be no question that their relationship was
over and neither of them wanted to reopen it. But
because of their damned unpredictable attraction, she had to worry about how *she* would react
around him. Not that she wanted to sleep with
him, but he'd seduced her before. And they were
about to spend hours alone. If she was lucky,
Cain would already be in the shower.

She swallowed. Best not to think about the
shower.

But as she stepped out of her car into the muggy
night, she realized it was much better to think of
him being away from her, upstairs in his room,

ignoring her as she cleaned, rather than close enough to touch, close enough to tempt, close enough to be tempted.

Cain watched her get out of her car and start up the driveway and opened the front door for her. "Come in this way."

She stepped into the echoing foyer with a tight, professional smile.

She was wary of him. Well, good. He was wary of her, of what was happening between them. It was bad enough to be attracted to someone he couldn't have. Now he was melting around her, doing her bidding when she looked at him with her big green eyes. He'd already decided the cure for his behavior around her was to treat her like an ex-wife. But he knew so little about her—except what he knew from their marriage—that he wasn't quite sure how to do that, either.

When he'd finally figured out they needed to get to know each other as the people they were now, he'd had Ava call with the request that Liz clean up after his dinner party. Maybe a little time spent alone would give them a chance to interact and she'd tell him enough about herself that he'd see her as a new person, or at least see her in a different light so he'd stop seeing the woman he'd loved every time he looked at her.

"Most of the mess is in the kitchen," he said, motioning for her to walk ahead of him. He didn't realize until she was already in front of him that that provided him with a terrific view of her backside and he nearly groaned, watching her jean-clad hips sway as she walked. This was why the part of him that wanted her back kept surfacing, taking control. Tonight the businessman had to wrestle control away.

"And the dining room." He said that as they entered his formal dining room and the cluttered table greeted them.

"I thought you were eating outside?"

"My bragging might have forced me to prove myself to the partners by being the chef for the steaks, but it was a formal meeting."

"Okay." She still wouldn't meet his gaze. "This isn't a big deal. You go ahead to your office or wherever. I can handle it. I've been here enough that I know where to put everything."

He shook his head. If they were going to be around each other for the next few weeks, they had to get to know each other as new people. Otherwise, they'd always relate to each other as the people they knew from their doomed marriage.

"It's late. If you do this alone, it could take hours. I'll help so you can be out of here before midnight."

The expression on her face clearly said she wanted to argue, but in the end, she turned and walked to the far side of the table, away from him. "Suit yourself."

She began stacking plates and gathering silverware at the head of the table. Cain did the same at the opposite end.

Though she hadn't argued with his decision to help her, she made it clear that she wasn't in the mood to talk. They worked in silence save for the clink and clatter of silverware and plates then he realized something amazing. She might be wary of him, but she wasn't afraid of his fancy silverware anymore. Wasn't afraid of chipping the china or breaking the crystal as she had been when they were married.

Funny that she had to leave him, become a maid, to grow accustomed to his things, his life-style.

"It seems weird to see how comfortable you are with the china."

She peeked up at him. "Until you said that, I'd forgotten how *uncomfortable* I had been around expensive things." She shrugged. "I was always afraid I'd break them. Now I can twirl them in the air and catch them behind my back with one hand."

He laughed, hoping to lighten the mood. "A demonstration's not really necessary."

She picked up a stack of dishes and headed for the kitchen.He grabbed some of the empty wine-glasses and followed her. If discussing his china was what it took to get her comfortable enough to open up, then he wasn't letting this conversation die. "I never did understand why you were so afraid."

"I'd never been around nice things."

"Really?" He shook his head in disbelief. "Liz, your job took you all over the place. You yourself told me that you had to wine and dine clients."

"In restaurants." She slid the glasses he handed her into the dishwasher. "It's one thing to go to a restaurant where somebody serves you and quite another to be the one in charge."

"You wouldn't hesitate now."

"No. I wouldn't. I love crystal and china and fancy silver."

The way he was watching her made Liz self-conscious, so embarrassed by her past that she felt the need to brag a little.

"I'm actually the person in charge of A Friend Indeed's annual fund-raiser." Her attention on placing dishes in the dishwasher, she added, "When we were married, I couldn't plan a simple Christmas party, now I'm in charge of a huge ball."

"There's a ball?"

Too late she realized her mistake. Though she wanted him to know about her accomplishments, she wasn't sure she wanted him at the ball, watching her, comparing her to the past. As coordinator for the event, she'd be nervous enough without him being there.

"It's no big deal," she said, brushing it off as insignificant. "Just Ayleen's way of getting her rich friends together to thank them for the donations she'll wheedle out of them before the end of the evening."

She straightened away from the dishwasher and headed for the dining room and the rest of the dirty dishes.

He followed her. "I know some people who could also contribute." He stopped in front of the table she was clearing and caught her gaze. "Can I get a couple of invitations to this ball or is it closed?"

Liz stifled a groan, as his dark eyes held hers. There was no way out of this.

"As someone working for the group, you're automatically invited. You won't get an invitation. Ayleen will simply expect you to be there."

But he would get invitations to Joni's barbecue and Matt's Christmas party. As long as he volunteered for A Friend Indeed, he'd be connected to her. She had to get beyond her fear that he would be watching her, evaluating her, remembering how she used to be.

The room became silent except for the clang of utensils as Liz gathered them. Cain joined in the gathering again. He didn't say anything, until they returned to the kitchen.

"Are you going to be uncomfortable having me there?"

She busied herself with the dishwasher to cover the fact that she winced. "No."

"Really? Because you seem a little standoffish. Weird. As if you're not happy that I want to go."

Because her back was to him, she squeezed her eyes shut. Memories of similar functions they'd attended during their marriage came tumbling back. Their compatibility in bed was only equaled by how incompatible they'd been at his events. A Friend Indeed's ball would be the first time he'd see her in his world since their divorce. She'd failed miserably when she was his wife. Now he'd see her in a gown, hosting the kind of event she'd refused to host for him.

"This *is* making you nervous." He paused, probably waiting for her to deny that. When she didn't he said, "Why?"

She desperately wanted to lie. To pretend nothing was wrong. But that was what had gotten her into trouble with him the first time around. She hadn't told him the truth about herself. She let him believe she was something she wasn't.

She sucked in a breath for courage and faced him. "Because I'll know you'll be watching me. Looking for the difference in how I am now and how I was when we were married."

He chuckled. "I've already noticed the differences."

"All the differences? I don't think so."

"So tell me."

"Maybe I don't want to be reminded of the past."

"Maybe if you told me about your past, you wouldn't be so afraid. If what you're fearing is my reaction, if you tell me, we'll get it out of the way and you won't have anything to fear anymore."

He wasn't exactly right, but he had made a point without realizing it. Maybe if she told him the truth about her humble beginnings and saw his disappointment, she could deal with it once and for all.

She returned to the dining room and walked around the table, gathering napkins as she spoke, so she wouldn't have to look at him.

"When I was growing up my mom just barely made enough for us to scrape by. I'd never even eaten in a restaurant other than fast food before I left home for university. I met you only one year out of school. And though by then I'd been wining and dining clients, traveling and seeing how the other half lived, actually being dumped into your lifestyle was culture shock to me."

"I got that—a little late, unfortunately—but I

got it. We were working around it, but you never seemed to adapt."

"That's because there's something else. Something that you don't know."

Also gathering things from the table, he stopped, peered over at her.

Glad for the distance between them, the buffer of space, she sucked in a fortifying breath. "I… um…my parents' divorce was not a happy one."

"Very few divorces are."

"Actually my mom, sisters and I ran away from my dad." She sucked in another breath. "He was abusive."

"He hit you?" Anger vibrated through his words, as if he'd demand payback if she admitted it was true.

"Yes. But he mostly hit my mom. We left in the night—without telling him we were going—because a charity like A Friend Indeed had a home for us hundreds of miles away in Philadelphia. We changed our names so my dad couldn't find us."

He sat on one of the chairs surrounding the

table. "Oh." Processing that, he said nothing for a second then suddenly glanced up at her. "You're not Liz Harper?"

"I am now. My name was legally changed over a decade ago when we left New York."

"Wow." He rubbed his hand along the back of his neck. "I'm sorry."

"It's certainly not your fault that my father was what he was or that I lived most of my life in poverty, always on the outside looking in, or that I didn't have the class or the experiences to simply blend into your life."

"That's why you're so attached to A Friend Indeed."

She nodded. "Yes."

A few seconds passed in silence. Liz hadn't expected him to say anything sympathetic. That simply wasn't Cain. But saying nothing at all was worse than a flippant reply. She felt the sting of his unspoken rejection. She wasn't good enough for him. She'd always known it.

"Why didn't you tell me before?"

She snorted a laugh. "Tell my perfect, handsome, wealthy husband who seemed to know everything that I was a clueless runaway? For as much as I loved you, I never felt I deserved you."

He smiled ruefully. "I used to think the same thing about you."

Disbelief stole her breath. Was he kidding her? She'd been the one with the past worth hiding. He'd been nothing but perfect. Maybe too perfect. "Really?"

"I would think why does this beautiful woman stay with me, when I'm an emotional cripple." He combed his fingers through his hair as if torn between the whole truth and just enough to satisfy her openmouthed curiosity. Finally he said, "The guilt of my brother's death paralyzed me. Even now, it sometimes sneaks up on me. Reminding me that if I'd left a minute sooner or a few seconds later, Tom would still be alive."

"The kid who hit you ran a red light. The accident wasn't your fault."

"Logically, I know that. But something deep inside won't let me believe it." He shook his head and laughed miserably. "I'm a fixer, remember.

Even after Tom's death, it was me Dad turned to for help running the business and eventually finding a replacement he could trust with his company when he wanted to retire. Yet, I couldn't fix that accident. I couldn't change any of it."

"No one could."

He snorted a laugh. "No kidding."

A few more seconds passed in silence. Fear bubbled in her blood. She had no idea why he'd confided in her, but she could see the result of it. She longed to hug him. To comfort him. But if she did that and they fell into bed, what good would that do but take them right back to where they had been? Solving all their problems with sex.

She grabbed her handful of napkins and walked them to the laundry room, realizing that rather than hug him, rather than comfort him, what she should be doing is airing all their issues. This conversation had been a great beginning, and this was probably the best opportunity she'd ever get to slide their final heartbreak into a discussion.

She readied herself, quickly assembling the

right words to tell him about their baby as she stepped out of the pantry into the kitchen again.

Cain stood by the dishwasher, arranging the final glasses on the top row. She took a deep breath, but before she could open her mouth, he said, "Do you know you're the only person I've ever talked about my brother's accident with?"

"You haven't talked with your family?"

He shrugged and closed the dishwasher door. Walking to the center island, he said, "We talk about Tom, but we don't talk about his accident. We talk about the fact that he's dead, but we never say it was my fault. My family has a wonderful way of being able to skirt things. To talk about what's palatable and avoid what's not."

Though he tried to speak lightly, she heard the pain in his voice, the pain in his words, the need to release his feelings just by getting some of this out in the open.

This was not the time to tell him about their baby. Not when he was so torn up about the accident. He couldn't handle it right now. Her brain told her to move on. She couldn't stand here and listen, couldn't let him confide, not even as a friend.

But her heart remembered the three sad, awful years after the accident and desperately wanted to see him set free.

"Do you want to talk about it now?"

He tossed a dishtowel to the center island. "What would I say?"

She caught his gaze. "I don't know. What would you say?"

"Maybe that I'm sorry?"

"Do you really think you need to say you're sorry for an accident?"

He smiled ruefully. "I guess that's the rub. I feel guilty about something that wasn't my fault. Something I can't change. Something I couldn't have fixed no matter how old, or smart or experienced I was."

"That's probably what's driving the fixer in you crazy."

"Yeah."

"It's not your fault. You can't be sorry." She shook her head. "No. You *can* be sorry your brother is gone. You can be sorry for the loss. But you can't take the blame for an accident."

"I know." He rubbed his hand along the back of his neck. "That was weird."

"Talking about it?"

"No, admitting out loud for the first time that it wasn't my fault. That I can't take the blame." He shook his head. "Wow. It's like it's the first time that's really sunk in."

He smiled at her, a relieved smile so genuine that she knew she'd done the right thing in encouraging him to talk.

The silence in the room nudged her again, hinting that she could now tell him about their baby, but something about the relieved expression on his face stopped her. He'd just absolved himself from a burden of guilt he never should have taken up. What if she told him about her miscarriage and instead of being sad, he got angry with himself all over again?

She swallowed, as repressed memories of the days before she left him popped up in her brain. All these years, she'd thought she'd kept her secret to protect herself. Now, she remembered that she'd also kept it to protect him. He had a talent for absorbing blame that wasn't really his.

If she told him now, with the conversation about his brother still lingering in the air, he could tumble right back to the place he'd just escaped. Surely he deserved a few days of peace? And surely in those days she could think of a way to tell him that would help him to accept, as she had, that there was no one to blame.

"We're just about finished here." She ambled to the dining room table again and brought back salt-and-pepper shakers. "I'll wash the tablecloth and wait for the dishwasher, but you don't have to hang around. I brought a book to read while I wait. Why don't you go do whatever you'd normally do?"

"I should pack the contracts we signed tonight in my briefcase."

"Okay. You go do that." She smiled at him. "I'll see you Friday morning."

He turned in the doorway. "I'm not supposed to be here when you come to the house, remember?"

She held his gaze. "I could come early enough to get a cup of coffee."

Surprise flitted across his face. "Really?" Then he grimaced. "I'm leaving town tomorrow morning. I won't be back until Friday night. But I'll see you on Saturday."

Another weekend of working with him without being able to tell him might be for the best. A little distance between tonight's acceptance that he couldn't take blame for his brother's accident and the revelation of a tragedy he didn't even know had happened wouldn't be a bad thing.

"Okay."

He turned to leave again then paused, as if he didn't want to leave her, and she realized she'd given him the wrong impression when she'd suggested they have coffee Friday morning. She'd suggested it to give herself a chance to tell him her secret, not because she wanted to spend time with him. But he didn't know that.

She turned away, a silent encouragement for him to move on. When she turned around again, he was gone.

CHAPTER SEVEN

THE FOLLOWING SATURDAY, Cain was on the roof of Amanda's house with a small crew of his best, most discreet workers. Even before Cain arrived, Liz had taken Amanda and her children to breakfast, then shopping, then to the beach. If he didn't know how well-timed this roof event had to be, he might have thought she was avoiding him.

Regret surged through him as he climbed down the ladder. He'd been so caught up in the fact that their talk had allowed him to pierce through the layer of guilt that had held him captive, that he'd nearly forgotten what she'd told him about her dad.

She'd been abused. She'd been raised in poverty. She'd run away, gotten herself educated in spite of her humble beginnings, and then she'd met him.

Their relationship could have gone one of two ways. He could have brought her into his world, shown her his lifestyle and gradually helped her acclimate. Instead, he'd fallen victim to the grief of his brother's death and missed the obvious.

He wanted to be angry with himself, but he couldn't. Just as he couldn't bear the burden of guilt over his brother's death, he couldn't blame himself for having missed the obvious. Blaming himself for things he couldn't change was over. But so was the chance to "fix" their marriage.

Somehow or another, that conversation over his dirty dishes had shown him that he and Liz weren't destined for a second chance. He could say that without the typical sadness over the loss of what might have been because he'd decided they hadn't known each other well enough the first time around to have anything to fix. What they really needed to do was start over.

He went through the back door into Amanda's kitchen, got a drink of water and then headed upstairs to assess what was left to be done, still thinking about him and Liz. The question was…

what did start over mean? Start over to become friends? Or start over to become lovers? A couple? A *married* couple?

He'd been considering them coworkers, learning to get along as friends for the sake of their project. But after the way she'd led him out of his guilt on Wednesday night, his feelings for her had shifted in an unexpected way. He supposed this was the emotion a man experienced when he found a woman who understood him, one he'd consider making his wife. The first time around his idea of a wife had been shallow. He'd wanted a beautiful hostess and someone to warm his bed. He'd never thought he'd need a confidante and friend more.

Now he knew just how wrong he'd been.

And now he saw just how right Liz would have been for him, if they'd only opened up to each other the first time around.

So should he expand his idea from experimenting with getting to know each other in order to become friends, to experimenting with getting to know each other to see if they actually were compatible? Not in the shallow ways, but in the real ways that counted.

Just the thought sent his head reeling. He didn't want to go back to what they'd had before...but a whole new relationship? The very idea filled him with a funny, fuzzy feeling. Though he didn't have a lot of experience with this particular emotion...he thought it just might be hope.

They couldn't fix their past. But what if they could have a future?

Shaking his head at the wonder of it all, Cain ducked into the first bedroom, the room with the most ceiling damage. He pulled a small notebook and pen from his shirt pocket and began making notes of things he would do the next day, Sunday. His crew would have the new roof far enough along that he could fix this ceiling and then the room could be painted. Because Amanda couldn't be there when any work crew was on site—to keep her identity safe—Liz would paint this room herself. The following weekend he and Billy could get to work on the baseboards and trim.

Proud of himself, Cain left the first room and walked into the second. This room still needed the works: ceiling, paint job, trim. He ducked out and into the bathroom, which was old-fashioned, but in good repair because he had fixed both the commode and shower the first week he'd been here. He dipped out and headed for the biggest bedroom, the one Amanda was using.

He stepped inside, only to find Liz stuffing a pillow into a bright red pillowcase.

"What are you doing here?"

Hand to her heart, she whipped around. "What are you doing down here! You're supposed to be on the roof."

"I'm making a list of things that need to be done tomorrow and next weekend."

"I'm surprising Amanda. I dropped her and her kids off at the beach, telling them I'd be back around six."

He leaned against the doorjamb. This room hadn't sustained any damage because of the bad roof. At some point during the week, Liz and Amanda had already painted the ceiling and walls. At the bottom of the bed were packages of new sheets and a red print comforter. Strewn across a mirror vanity were new curtains—red-and-gold striped that matched the colors in the comforter—waiting to be installed.

"By giving her a whole new bedroom?"

"Having a bedroom that's a comfortable retreat is a simple pleasure." Shaking a second pillow into a pillowcase, she smiled. "Women like simple pleasures. Bubble baths. A fresh cup of coffee. A good book."

"And a pretty bedroom."

She nodded. "And before you ask, Amanda's favorite color is red. I'm not going overboard."

"I'm glad because another person might consider this whole system a bit bright."

"This from a man with a black satin bedspread."

He laughed. "Point taken."

"How's the roof going?"

"It'll be done tomorrow night. That's the good thing about these houses. Small, uncomplicated roofs."

"Good."

With the pillows now on the bed and the fitted sheet in place, Liz grabbed the flat sheet, unfurling it over the bed.

Cain strode over and caught the side opposite her. "Here. Let me help."

"Thanks."

"You're welcome." He paused then added, "You know I'm really proud of you, right?"

"You don't have to say that."

"I think I do. Wednesday night, we sort of skipped from your childhood to my brother's death and never got back to it."

"There's no need."

"I think there is." He hesitated. In for a penny, in for a pound. "I'd like to know more." He shook his head. "No. That's not right. You said it's not something you want to talk about." In three years of living together, he'd bet she'd shown him signs of her troubles, but he'd never seen. He regretted now that he'd never seen her pain. Deeply. Wholeheartedly. If he'd noticed, he could have asked her about it at any time in their marriage.

Now he knew she wanted it to be put behind her. If he really wanted a clean slate, he had to accept what she wanted, too.

"What I'm trying to say is that I want you to know that I get it. I understand. And maybe I'm sorry."

He still wasn't sure what he intended to do. If he should trust that funny feeling in the pit of his stomach that told him he should pursue this. Mostly because she was so different now that he had to treat her differently. She had goals and dreams. The first time they'd met he'd pulled her away from everything she had and everything she wanted. He wouldn't do that to her this time.

And maybe that was the real test of whether or not they belonged together. If he could coexist without taking over, and if she could keep her independence without letting him overpower her, then maybe they did belong together.

He nearly snorted with derision. That was a tall order for a man accustomed to being the boss and a woman so obviously eager to please.

"You don't have to be sorry."

"Well, I am. I'm sorry I didn't put two and two together. I'm sorry I made things worse."

They didn't speak while finishing the bed. Liz couldn't have spoken if she'd tried. There was a lump in her throat so thick she couldn't have gotten words past it.

When the bed was all set up, he said, "I better get back to the roof."

Liz nodded, smiling as much as she could, and he left the room. She watched him go then forced her attention on the bed she'd just made. She'd missed another really good opportunity to tell him. But his apology about her situation with her dad had left her reeling. She hadn't wanted to be overly emotional when she told him about their lost child. She wanted to be strong. So he could be sad. She wanted to keep the focus of the discussion on the loss being a loss…not someone's fault.

Still, she'd better pick a time…and soon. With two honest discussions under their belts, he'd wonder why she'd kept her most important secret to herself when she'd had opportunities to tell him.

The following weekend and the weekend after, Liz found herself working primarily with Amanda. With the roof done, Amanda and Billy didn't need to be off premises, and both were eager to get back on the job. Cain and Billy did the "man's work" as Billy called it, and Amanda and Liz painted and then made lunches. There was never a time when she and Cain were alone.

Their final Sunday of work, with the roof replaced, the rooms painted, the plumbing working at peak efficiency, and shiny new baseboard and crown molding accenting each room, Amanda had wanted to make a big celebration dinner, but Cain had a conference call and Liz had begged off in favor of a cold shower. She kissed Amanda, Joy and Billy's cheeks as Cain shook hands and gave hugs, then both headed for their vehicles.

"That was amazing," Cain said when they were far enough from Amanda's house that she couldn't hear.

Liz blew out a breath of relief. "Dear God, yes. Finishing is amazing!"

He shook his head. "No. I'm talking about actually doing something for someone." He sighed, stopping at the door to his truck. "You know that I give hundreds of thousands of dollars away a year, so you know I'm not a slouch. But giving is one thing. Working to help make a real person's life better is entirely different."

"No kidding!"

"I don't think you're hearing what I'm telling you. I feel terrific."

She laughed. "You've got charity worker's high."

He shook his head again. "No. It's more than that. I feel like I've found my new calling."

Shielding her eyes from the sun, she peeked up at him, finally getting what he was telling her. "Really?"

"Yes."

"You know A Friend Indeed has other houses."

"Yes."

"You can call Ayleen and I'm sure she'll let you fix any one of them you want."

He caught her gaze. "Will you help?"

Her heart stopped. Spend another several weeks with him? "I don't know." She pulled in a breath. When he looked at her with those serious eyes of his, she couldn't think of saying no. Especially since he'd been so happy lately. And especially since she still had something to tell him and needed to be around him.

But she didn't really want to connect their lives, and working together on another project more or less made them a team.

"Okay, while you think about that, answer this. I'm considering hiring Billy to be my assistant on these jobs. I know I'll have to clear it with Ayleen, but before I talk to her I'd like a little background. Just enough that I don't push any wrong buttons."

"As long as you don't hit his mother, I think you'll be fine."

"That bad, huh?"

Liz sighed. "I think the real problem might be getting him to accept a job."

"Really? Why?"

"He might think it's charity."

"I never thought of that."

"He's got a lot of pride."

Cain snorted a laugh. "No kidding. But we made headway working together." He grinned at her. "I think he likes me."

Liz rolled her eyes. "He admires you."

"So I'll use that. I'll tell him he's getting a chance to work with the big dog. Learn the secrets of my success."

She laughed and an odd warmth enveloped her. Talking with him now was like talking with Ellie. Casual. Easy. Maybe they really had become friends?

"Hey, you never know. It might work."

She grimaced. "I'm sure it will work." She finished the walk to her car. She didn't mind being friends with him, but she also didn't want to risk the feeling going any further.

As she opened the door, Cain called after her, "So, are you going to help me?"

That was the rub. If she agreed to work with him, they really would become friends. And she'd probably have plenty of time not only to tell him her secret, but also to help him adjust to it. On the flip side, if things didn't go well, she'd have plenty of time to see him angry, to watch him mourn, if he didn't handle the news well.

"I'm going to think about it."

Liz slid into her car and drove away. Cain opened his truck door. He'd expected her to be happier that he wanted to work on more houses. But he supposed in a way he understood why she wasn't. The very reason he wanted her to work with him—to be together, to spend time together so they could get to know each other and see if they shouldn't start over again—might be the reason she didn't want to work with him. Their marriage had been an abysmal failure. She didn't want to be reminded and she didn't want to go back.

If he was considering "fixing" their marriage,

he'd be as negative as she was. But he didn't want to fix their marriage. He wanted them to start over again.

Unfortunately, he wasn't entirely sure how.

Tuesday, Cain spoke with Ayleen and got approval to hire Billy. Actually, he got gushing glowing praise on the job he had done and his generosity in taking Billy under his wing. Then he got the address of the next house he was to repair and the suggestion that he might want to start that Saturday.

So he drove to Amanda's and offered Billy a job, which Billy happily accepted, especially after Cain mentioned his salary.

High on the success of the first part of his plan, Cain called Liz the minute he returned to his house.

She answered on the first ring. "Happy Maids."

"You really should have a personal cell phone."

"Can't afford it. What do you want, Cain?"

"Is that any way to talk to the man who's offering you a ride to our job site on Saturday?

I'm already stopping for Billy—one more will fit into the truck."

"You got Billy to take a job?"

"I made him an offer he couldn't refuse."

"That's great! Amanda will be so thrilled."

"I'm glad to be able to do it." He paused. "So what do you say? Want a ride?"

"I haven't even agreed to work with you yet."

He could have threatened her with calling Ayleen and forced her hand. He could have said, "Please," and maybe melted her the way she could melt him. Instead he said nothing, letting the decision be her own, following his own directive that this relationship would be totally different. Fresh. New.

"Okay. But I'll meet you there." Her answer was cool, businesslike, but he didn't care. They'd had a crappy marriage. He'd hurt her. But more than that, he'd pulled her away from her dreams. He had to accept that she'd be wary of him. Then he had to prove to her she had no reason to be. They were starting over.

* * *

Peggy Morris had chosen not to be home when Cain and company did the work on her house. Liz had said she would get the keys and be there when Cain and Billy arrived. As Cain opened the back door into the kitchen, she turned from the sink. When she saw the picnic basket Billy carried, she grinned.

"Your mom's a saint."

Billy frowned. "Why?"

"For making lunch."

"I made that," Cain said. "Well, actually, I had Ava call a deli and place an order. I've got sandwiches, soda, bottled water, dessert… The cheesecake you like."

She groaned. "Oh, Cain! I can't have cheesecake! I'll be big as a house."

He laughed. She might have groaned about the cheesecake, but she accepted that he'd brought lunch. It was a good start. "You've lost weight since we were married."

Billy glanced from Cain to Liz. "You two were married?"

Cain said, "Yes."

Liz said, "A long time ago."

Billy shook his head. "You don't look like married people to me."

Liz walked over and put her hand on Billy's forearm. "Your parents' situation wasn't normal, Billy."

"Yeah, but even my friends' parents argue all the time. You two get along." He looked from Cain to Liz again. "So why'd you get divorced?"

"Long story," Liz said.

"I was too busy," Cain countered.

Before Billy could say anything more about them, Liz turned him in the direction of the door again. "You don't need to know about this. It's ancient history, and we do need to get started on what we came here to do." She pointed at the door. "I'm guessing Cain's got about ten cans of paint in his truck. Let's go get them."

The three of them made a good team. Liz jumped into the truck bed and handed paint gallons, brushes, trays and other equipment to Cain and Billy who carted everything into the garage.

When the supplies were on the garage floor, Cain took charge again. "We're starting at this house because essentially everything is in good repair. When Ayleen brought me over this week to check things out, I noticed a few of the walls and ceilings need to be mended and there's also some work in the bathroom." He pointed at a new shower head and some unidentifiable plumbing equipment in another package. "I'll do all that. You guys can paint. I thought we'd start upstairs and work our way downstairs."

Liz said, "Okay."

Billy said, "I already know how to paint. I want to help with the repair work."

"The thing about construction is that you have to do whatever needs to be done. You don't get to pick your job." He handed Billy two gallons of beige paint. "Eventually you'll demonstrate that you have a strength or two like electrical or plumbing, and you'll be considered the expert and get to do those jobs whenever they come up. But if there's no electrical or plumbing, you'll paint."

Billy grumbled, but Cain pretended not to notice. Hiding a smile, Liz picked up some paint trays, brushes and rollers and followed Billy to the door into the kitchen.

He waited until Billy was through the door before he called her back. "Liz?"

She turned, her eyes wide and round, as if afraid of what he might say.

He wanted to tell her thanks. He wanted to say she looked pretty that morning. Because she appeared to be afraid of him and his motives, he handed the blue tape to her. "You're not a good enough painter to forget the blue tape."

She didn't have a free hand, so he tossed it onto a paint tray, then turned and picked up the bag of plaster.

Liz spent an enjoyable morning painting with Billy. A few times Cain came into the room and either pulled Billy to show him something about the repair work he was doing on the ceiling or in the bathroom, or to praise them for the good job they were doing. Billy blossomed under Cain's attention. He even chattered to Liz about the toilet tank "guts" exchange that Cain had explained to him.

"Because it's normal for commodes to need these kinds of repairs," Billy repeated Cain's comments verbatim. "My mom might need me to do that one day."

Though Liz was tempted to laugh, she held it back. "That's right. If you learn enough with Cain, you'll be able to fix things as they break at home."

"I know," Billy said seriously, sounding proud and responsible.

Liz ruffled his hair. "Get your paintbrush. We've got hours of this ahead of us."

Lunch was fun and relaxing. Billy had a million questions for Cain and he happily answered them. Having completed the repair work to the walls and ceilings, Cain joined the painting in the afternoon.

At five, Liz suggested they begin cleaning up.

"I could go for another hour or two, how about you, Billy?"

"I'm cool."

Liz shook her head. "The family has to come home sometime. Because Peggy is new and doesn't know any of us, Ayleen doesn't want her to find us here when she returns."

"Oops." Cain laughed. "Forgot."

Leaving the paint and supplies in the garage, Cain and Billy piled into his truck again. Liz walked to her car.

"See you tomorrow?"

She faced the truck. "Yeah."

Cain grinned at her. "Okay."

She climbed into her car with the same strange feeling she'd had at Amanda's about Cain being normal. Wondering if he was working to make her a friend or trying to ease her back into a relationship. But this time it was slightly different. Dealing with him today had been like dealing with a new friend. A *new* friend. Which was odd.

She knew their discussion about his brother had released him from the burden of guilt that had held him back emotionally. He was happy now. Easygoing. Which was probably why he seemed like a new person to her. She was also grateful that she had helped him. But something new was entering their equation. A question. A problem.

What if she told him about their baby and it threw him into a tailspin again?

She turned and watched his truck as it roared down the road. Billy sat in the passenger's side, his elbow out the open window. Cain sat in the driver's side, his elbow out the open window. They could be friends. Older and younger brother.

The truck turned right and disappeared down the street. Liz watched after it. He couldn't fake what he felt for Billy. The boy was just a tad too inquisitive for an impatient man like Cain to fake patience. He was the happiest she'd ever seen him. And her secret could ruin that.

The next morning Cain arrived at the house with Billy in tow and another picnic basket stuffed with food. Eager for lunch, Billy went straight to work. He'd become so good at painting and had such a steady hand that Cain suggested he paint the line bordering the ceiling and around the windows and trim.

Proud of himself, Billy continued to blossom under the praise.

But Liz found herself watching Cain, watching his patience with Billy, watching his commitment to doing a good job for A Friend Indeed, watching the way he treated her. Not as an ex-wife, not as a woman he was pursuing, but as a coworker.

In a lot of ways that was weird.

"Get the lead out, Harper. If you keep repainting the same wall, we'll be here again next weekend."

"Got it. Sorry."

"If you're tired, take a break."

She faced him. "A break? What's a break? Billy, do you know what a break is?"

"Not hardly."

She laughed and went back to painting, but Cain sighed. "All right. We'll all take ten minutes then we have to get back to it."

Liz didn't need to be told twice. After using the bathroom, she jogged down the stairs and into the garage, where Cain had stored a cooler with bottled water and soft drinks. She took a can of diet cola, snapped open the lid and drank.

"Sorry about that."

Lowering the can from her mouth, she turned and saw Cain walking into the garage. "You don't have to go overboard with being nice."

"I'm not."

"Sure you are. I'll bet you wouldn't apologize to your workers if you got so wrapped up in a job you forgot to give them a break."

"Probably not."

"So why treat me and Billy any differently?"

"Maybe because I'm having trouble finding a happy medium."

"Billy's a good kid who needs to be in the real world. And that might include a boss who forgets to give him a break."

"I'm not having trouble figuring out how to deal with Billy."

Right. She got it. She was the problem. Their feelings around each other had gone up and down, back and forth and sideways. Plus they had a past. Even as objective as she tried to be, sometimes that past snuck up on her.

"Maybe that's because we shouldn't be working together."

Just when she thought he'd admit he'd made a mistake in asking for her help, he surprised her. "We both like Billy. We both recognize that if somebody doesn't grab hold of him right now God only knows what he'll get into." He caught her gaze. "We can do this, Liz. We can help him. Save him. Don't you even want to try?"

She swallowed. "Actually, I do." And for the first time since she'd seen him standing in only a towel in his kitchen, she wanted to tell *him* she was proud of *him*. She wanted to say it so much that she suddenly understood what he'd been going through every time he'd seen one of the changes she'd made since their marriage.

The feeling was nearly overwhelming.

"You know I'll help Billy. I'll do everything I can."

He smiled at her, a smile so warm and open, she could only stare at him. The spark was back in his dark brown eyes. His hair fell boyishly to his forehead. But that smile. Oh, that smile. She would have done anything to see that smile three years ago. It seemed to say that he was different. Happy. Easy to be around. If they didn't have a past, if she didn't have a secret, Cain would be the man she would actually consider giving her heart to.

But they did have a past. And she did have a secret.

She chugged her soda and headed into the house just as Billy came out.

"Hey! I didn't even get a drink."

"Go ahead and get one. I'm ready to get back to work, so I'm going in. You and Cain take all the time you need."

CHAPTER EIGHT

CAIN JUMPED INTO his Porsche and punched the address on the invitation in his hand into his GPS unit. He'd been invited to a party being hosted by one of the women who'd been helped by A Friend Indeed. In a few minutes, he found himself driving down the street of the middle-class, blue-collar neighborhood.

He hadn't wanted to attend this party. But it had been a real stretch for him to volunteer to help with the Friend Indeed houses and an even bigger stretch to have taken Billy under his wing and those things had worked out amazingly well. So attending an event for the families involved with the charity was simply another level of change for him. Especially since it would involve chitchat. No bankers or businessmen to schmooze.

No business talk tonight. Somehow or other he'd have to be...well, normal.

But he'd decided to once again push beyond his own inadequacies to attend tonight because he couldn't stop thinking about something Liz had told him. When he'd first arrived at Amanda's, Liz had instructed him to accept anything any client offered because this might be the first time in a long time they'd had something to offer. He'd finally wrapped his head around just how demoralized and demeaned these women had been and then his thoughts had segued to the fact that Liz and her family had been abused.

Liz had been a child in a family just like this one. Alone. Scared. Usually hungry. He couldn't bear the thought.

But that also meant he couldn't refuse an invitation to anything connected to Liz. He didn't want her to feel rejected by him, or that somehow she and her friends weren't good enough. They were. He was the socially awkward one. So to protect her, here he was, driving in an unfamiliar section of the city, about to attend a gathering with people he didn't know.

He parked on the street and headed up the sidewalk to Joni Custer's house. As he climbed the stairs to the front door, he held back a wince of pain. He'd been so busy proving himself to Liz and enjoying doing the work he loved—the work that had nudged him in the direction of success and riches—that he'd forgotten he wasn't eighteen anymore. Billy was probably stronger. And maybe he should be the one hefting boxes of hardwood, while Cain stuck to measuring and fitting.

He found the bell and within two seconds, the bright red front door opened. Liz stood on the other side. Dressed in shorts and a halter top, she looked amazing. Comfortable. Confident. Relaxed.

Their gazes caught and she smiled sheepishly. His heart did a cartwheel. She was smiling at him now, like a real person, not a person she was forced to socialize with, not a person she had to pretend to like. Her smile was genuine.

"Come on. Everybody's outside on the patio."
She took a look at his attire and winced. "Somebody should have told you dress was informal."

Cain immediately reached for his tie. Walking
into the foyer, he yanked it off and stuffed it in
his jacket pocket. "I can make do." He removed
his jacket and tossed it over a hook on a coat tree
in the foyer. Following Liz to a sliding glass door
at the back of the house, he rolled up the sleeves
of his white shirt. "See, now I'm dressed appropriately."

"Well, not exactly appropriately." She turned
and gave him another smile. "But better."

"How about a little background before I go out
there into a sea of people I don't know."

"Joni is one of the first women we helped.
Every year she hosts a barbecue. Most of the people attending are also A Friend Indeed women,
but some are parents and friends of the clients."
She hooked her arm in the crook of his elbow
and headed for the door again. "I'll introduce you
around, but then you're on your own."

It felt so good to have her at his side that it disappointed him that she wouldn't stay with him, but he understood. If they had just met, they'd still be in a friend stage, not behaving like a couple. He had to accept that.

"I appreciate the introductions."

She hesitated another few seconds at the door. "You might get a critique or two of the work you've done."

"Hey, you helped!" He opened the sliding glass door. "If I'm going down in flames, you're going with me."

She laughed and the second they stepped onto the stone floor of the small patio, Liz said, "Hey, everybody, this is Cain. He's the new board member who's been fixing up houses."

A general round of approval rippled through the crowd.

Liz leaned in and whispered, "Get ready. Any second now you'll be surrounded."

Her warning didn't penetrate. He was too busy analyzing whether it was good or bad that she hadn't introduced him as her ex-husband. On the one hand it did point to the fact that she saw their association as being a new one. On the other, she could be embarrassed about having been married to him. So it took him by surprise when a middle-aged man approached him and extended his hand for shaking.

"You did Amanda's house?"

"That was mostly painting," Cain said, snatching Liz's hand, holding her in place when it appeared she would desert him. "And Liz and I were equal partners on that one."

"Don't be so modest," Ayleen said, ambling up to them. "I hear the whole house is to die for."

"It is." Amanda walked over. She unexpectedly hugged Cain. "Thanks again."

Embarrassment flooded him at her praise. What he'd done was so simple, so easy for him. Yet it had meant the world to Amanda. "I guess that means you like the house?"

"*Like* is too simple of a word," she said with a laugh.

Liz shook her hand free of his, as if eager to get away. "How about if I get us a drink? What would you like?"

Not quite sure what to say, Cain raised his eyebrows in question. "What do they have?"

"What if I get us both a cola?"

"Sounds great."

The second Liz left, he began fielding questions about the work he'd done on Amanda's house and the four houses he still planned to repair.

Eventually he and the middle-aged man who introduced himself as Bob, Joni's dad, wandered over to the grill.

"This is my grandson, Tony." Bob introduced Cain to the man flipping burgers.

Cain caught a flash of yellow out of his peripheral vision before a tall blonde grabbed his forearm and yanked him away from the grill. "Sorry, guys. But he's mine for a few minutes." She smiled at him. "I'm Ellie. My friends call me Magic."

"Magic? Like Magic Johnson, the basketball player?"

"No, magic as in my wishes generally come true and I can also pretty much figure out somebody's deal in a short conversation."

"You're going to interrogate me, aren't you?"

"I know who you are."

"Who I am?"

"You're Liz's ex. She hasn't said anything, but for her to be introducing you around, I'm guessing she likes you again."

He paused. His heart skipped a beat. Her wariness around him took on new meaning. He'd been so careful to behave only as a friend that she might not understand his feelings for her now ran much deeper. She might think he didn't like her "that" way anymore. But he did. And if she wanted more, so did he.

"Really?"

Ellie sighed. "Really. Come on. Let's cut the bull. We both know you're cute. We both know she loved you. Now you're back and she's falling for you. If she's holding back, I'm guessing it's only because she thinks you don't want her."

Cain couldn't help it; he smiled.

Ellie shook her head with a sigh. "Don't be smug. Or too sure of yourself. As her friend, I'm going to make it my business to be certain you don't hurt her again."

"You don't have to make it your business. You have my word."

She studied his face. "Odd as this is going to sound, I believe you."

Liz walked over with two cans of cola. "Ellie! What are you doing?"

"Checking him out," Ellie said without an ounce of shame in her voice. "I'm going to help Joni with the buns and salads."

Liz faced him with a grimace. "Sorry about that."

"Is she really magic?"

Liz laughed. "Did she tell you that?"

"Yes."

"Then she likes you and that's a big plus."

Liz casually turned to walk away, but Cain caught her arm. "So these people are your friends?"

"Yes."

He expected her to elaborate, but she didn't. She eased her arm out of his grasp and walked away. Ten minutes ago, that would have upset him. Now, Ellie's words repeated in his head. "If she's holding back I'm guessing it's only because she thinks you don't want her."

He glanced around and frowned. They were with her friends. He couldn't make a move of any kind here. That much *he* was sure of. But soon, very soon, he was going to have to do something to test Ellie's theory.

Cain went back to the group of men at the grill and in seconds he felt odd. Not exactly uncomfortable. Not exactly confused. But baffled, as if something important sat on the edge of his brain trying to surface but it couldn't.

The conversation of the men around him turned to children, house payments and job difficulties. He couldn't identify with anything they were discussing. He didn't have kids or a mortgage or job difficulties. So, he didn't say a word, simply listened, putting things in context by remembering the things he'd learned working with Billy and for Amanda, and then he suddenly understood why he felt so weird.

It wasn't because Liz's magical friend had basically told him that Liz cared for him. It was because Liz had left him alone with her friends. Alone. Not monitoring what he said. Not anxious or fearful that he'd inadvertently insult someone.

She trusted him.

She *trusted* him.

Just the thought humbled him. But also sort of proved out Ellie's suspicion that Liz liked him again as more than a friend. A woman didn't trust the people she loved to just anyone.

When the burgers were grilled to perfection, Cain scooped them up with a huge metal spatula and piled them on a plate held by Bob. When everything was on the table, he took a seat at the picnic table where Liz sat. He didn't sit beside her. He didn't want to scare her, but he did like being around her. And Ellie's comment that Liz was falling for him again was beginning to settle in, to give him confidence, to make him think that maybe it was time to let her know he was feeling the same way she was.

Not that it was time to get back together, but to start over.

The group at each table included adults of all ages and varieties and their children. They ate burgers, discussed football and fishing, and when everyone had eaten their fill, they played volleyball—in spite of Cain's Italian loafers. When the sun set, the kids disappeared to tell ghost stories in the dark, humid night and the adults congregated around the tables again, talking about everything from raising kids to the economy.

All in all it was a very relaxing evening, but an informative one, as well. Liz fit with these people. Easily. Happily.

And he had, too.

It was time for him to get their relationship on track. And since they were doing things differently this time around, he wouldn't slyly seduce her. He intended to actually tell her he wanted to be more than her friend, ask her if she agreed. To give her choices. To give her time.

Exactly the opposite of what he'd done when he met her six years ago.

The back door slid open. A little kid of about six yelled, "Hey! There's a jacket in here that's buzzing."

Everybody laughed.

An older girl raced up behind the kid. "Somebody's cell phone is vibrating. It's in the pocket of a jacket hanging on the coat tree."

Cain rose. He'd been so caught up in being with Liz that he'd forgotten his cell phone, hadn't cared if he missed a call. "I think that's mine." He glanced at Joni with a smile. "It's time for me to be going anyway. Thank you very much for inviting me."

Joni rose. "Thank you for coming. It was nice to meet the guy who's stirred up so much gossip!"

Not exactly sure how to take that, Cain faced Liz, who also rose. "She means about fixing the houses." She slid her hand in the crook of his elbow. "I'll walk you to the door."

Liz waited as Cain said his good-nights. Together they walked into the house and to the foyer. He lifted his suit jacket from the coat tree and the phone buzzed again. He silenced it without even looking at caller ID.

She nearly shook her head in wonder. She'd been worried about how he'd handle this party, how he'd get along with her friends, and she needn't have given it a second thought.

He opened the front door. "Walk me to my car?"

Her breath stuttered in her chest. If they hadn't had such a nice evening, she might have thought this was her perfect opportunity to tell him about their baby. But they had had a nice evening. A quiet, comfortable, relaxing time. She'd seen how hard he worked to get along with her friends. And she'd appreciated that. Her sad revelation was for another time.

She pulled her keys from her pocket. "How about if you walk *me* to *my* car?"

He smiled. "Sure. I just thought you'd be going back in."

"Nope."

"You know Ellie's going to give you the third degree. Might as well get it over with tonight."

"Not necessary. She'll call me before I even get home."

He laughed. Her chest constricted with happiness as unexpected feelings rippled through her. She hadn't fully admitted to herself how important it was to her that he like her friends. But it had been. Seeing him interacting with the Friend Indeed people had filled her with pride. She couldn't remember a time when he'd ever been this relaxed and she knew she'd had something to do with that. She'd helped him get beyond his guilt and helped him acclimate at A Friend Indeed, and in the end he'd become the man she'd always known he could be. Warm. Caring. Wonderful.

When they reached her atrocious little green car, she turned and faced him. Their gazes met and clung and she suddenly realized asking him to walk her to her car might have seemed like an invitation for him to kiss her good-night.

Her heart stilled. Her breathing stalled in her chest. Part of her screamed for her to grab the door handle and get the hell out of here. The other part was melting into soft putty. She'd loved this man with her whole heart and soul. He'd suffered the torment of the damned and she'd had to stand by helplessly. Now he was back. Almost normal, but better.

Was it so wrong to want one little kiss?

As his head slowly descended, she had a thousand chances to change her mind. A million cautions pirouetted through her brain. Every nerve ending in her body flickered with something that felt very much like fear.

But when their lips met, it was like coming home. The years melted away and he was the Cain she'd fallen in love with. Cain before he'd been burdened by guilt over his brother's death or the drive to succeed to bury that guilt.

The Cain she knew loved her.

He was *her* Cain.

Her lips came to life slowly beneath his. His hands slid to her upper arms, to her back and down her spine. She stepped closer, nestling against him. For the three years of their marriage she'd longed for this feeling. For the three years they'd been separated, she'd tried to forget this feeling. The warmth, the connection, the spark of need that ignited in her and heated her blood. Nobody had ever made her feel what Cain made her feel.

And she was finally discovering part of the reason was that she didn't want anybody else to make her feel what Cain could. She wanted Cain.

He pulled away slowly. She blinked up at him. "Good night."

His voice was a soft whisper in the warm summer night. Her lips curved upward slowly. A kiss. Just a kiss. He hadn't pushed for more, hadn't asked her to follow him home, or if he could follow her. He'd simply wanted a kiss.

"Good night."

"I'll call you."

"Okay."

She opened her car door and slid inside. He stepped back, out of the way, as she pulled her gearshift into Drive and eased out into the night.

A little voice inside her head told her not to

be so happy, because she hadn't yet been totally honest with him.

But she would be.

Soon.

For now though she wanted to bask in the warmth that flooded her because he'd kissed her.

Cain couldn't remember ever feeling so good or so hopeful about his life. It wasn't simply because Liz had feelings for him and had admitted them in the way she kissed him. He was also a changed man. He hadn't pretended to like her friends. He liked her friends. He hadn't been bored, nervous, or eager to get away to get back to work. Somehow or another over the past weeks, his longing to make up to Liz for their horrible marriage had reordered his priorities. He'd done what he felt he needed to do to pay penance for their bad marriage and as a result learned to work with Billy and for a cause that genuinely needed him.

And when the dust settled, he was changed. When he looked ahead to their future, he could see them making it work this time.

Driving home with the top down, thinking about some of the brighter days in their marriage, he almost didn't hear his cell phone ring. He'd shifted it from vibrate to ring when he directed the last call to voice mail as he'd walked Liz to her car. Though it had taken a few rings, eventually the low sound penetrated his consciousness and he grabbed the phone. Somebody had been trying to get a hold of him for the past hour, but he hadn't even cared enough to check caller ID.

If that didn't prove he'd changed, nothing did.

He glanced at the small screen and saw his sister's phone number.

His sister? What would be so important that she'd call at least three times on a Sunday night? He frowned and clicked the button to answer.

"What's up, sis?"

"Cain. Thank God you finally answered. Dad's on his way to the hospital. Mom thinks he had a heart attack. It's pretty bad."

All the good feelings welled in his belly turned into a rock of dread. Even if the words hadn't penetrated, the shiver in his sister's voice had.

"I'm on my way."

Without another thought, he pressed speed dial for Ava. Her voice groggy with sleep, she said, "Cain?"

"Sorry to wake you. My dad had a heart attack. I need to get to Kansas tonight. Can you wake Dale?" he asked, referring to his pilot.

"I'm on it," Ava said sounding awake and alert. "You just get yourself to the airport."

CHAPTER NINE

LIZ'S CELL PHONE was ringing when she awoke the next morning. She reached over and pawed the bedside table to snag it. When she saw the name on caller ID, her breath stuttered out.

Cain.

He'd kissed her the night before. She'd wanted him to. Her insides tightened at the memory. She'd always loved him and now he was behaving as if he loved her, too. Doing things for her. Caring about the cause she cared about. Easing his way into her life.

Part of her wanted it. All of it. The attention, the affection, the connection. The other part of her was scared to death. They'd made a mistake before.

Her phone rang again and she pressed the button to answer. Her voice was soft and uncertain when she said, "Good morning, Cain."

"Good morning."

His greeting was rough, tired, as if he hadn't slept all night. And not for good reasons.

She scrambled up in bed. "What's wrong?"

"My dad had a heart attack yesterday. I'm in Kansas."

She flopped back onto her pillow. "Oh, God. I'm so sorry. Is there anything I can do?"

"No, I just—" He paused. "I just—"

He paused again and Liz squeezed her eyes shut. She got it. He'd called her for support, but he couldn't say it. Didn't know how. He'd never asked anyone for support or help before.

Tears filled her eyes and her heart clenched. She'd longed for him to reach out to her in the three years of their marriage, but he hadn't been able to. Now, after coming to terms with his brother's death, after spending some time with her, he was finally turning to her.

How could she possibly not respond to that?

"Would you like me to fly to Kansas?"

He sucked in a breath. "No. You have a business to run and things here are out of our control. There's nothing you could do."

"I could hold your hand."

She said the words softly and wasn't surprised when he hesitated before he said, "Right now I'm holding my mother's hand."

"She needs you, Cain." And he hadn't thought twice about flying out to be with her. At his core, he'd always loved his family. He simply felt he'd let them down. "Is there anything I can do for you here?"

"You could call Ava, let her know there's no news but that I arrived safely."

She smiled. That little kindness was also something she wouldn't have expected from him three years ago—or three weeks ago.

"I'll be glad to." She paused then said, "If you'll call me any time there's news, I'll call her and keep her posted."

"Okay."

"Okay." She wanted to tell him she loved him. The words sat on her tongue aching to jump off.

He needed to hear it. She longed to say it. But what would happen when his dad was better and he came home? Would those three little words cause awkwardness, or push them beyond where they should be in this relationship they seemed to be building? Would it cause another mistake? Especially since love hadn't been enough the first time.

"I'll call you."

"Lucky for you you only have to remember one cell number."

He laughed. "Goodbye, Liz."

"Goodbye." She disconnected the call then sat staring at the phone. She'd said and done all the right things. She'd been supportive. He'd accepted her support. But they hadn't gone too far.

But he'd called *her*. Not his assistant. He'd been vulnerable with her in a way he'd never been before. He'd even asked her to make his phone call to Ava for him.

He was definitely different.

And she had a lot of thinking to do.

* * *

At noon, Ellie dropped into the Happy Maids' office with iced tea and sandwiches. "So dish! What happened?"

Liz looked up from the spreadsheet she was reading, as Ellie set the iced tea and sandwiches on her desk. "What happened when?"

"Last night. With your ex. I know you told me he was withdrawn after his brother's death, but it looks like he's getting over it and…" She nudged Liz across the desk. "He wants you back. Why else would a man play volleyball in those shoes he had on?"

Liz pulled in a big breath. "That's actually the problem. I think he does want us to get back together."

Ellie sat. "You say that as if it's bad."

"It was a crappy marriage. We both walked away hurt."

"Because he was closed off after his brother's death," Ellie insisted as she opened the bag and pulled out the sandwiches.

Accepting hers from Ellie, Liz said, "There's

a lot more to it than that. I didn't fit in with the businessmen and their wives that he socialized with. I couldn't plan his parties." Even as she said the words, Liz realized that would no longer be true. Just as she'd explained to Cain as they were cleaning up after his dinner party, she had grown. Changed. "And he had a tendency to disappear when he had an important project. I spent a lot of those three years alone."

"Things would be different this time," Ellie said before she bit into her sandwich. "Even a person without magic could see that. He's different. Involved. Interested." She peered across the desk at Liz. "And you're different."

"Which sort of makes my point. We're so different that we'd actually have to get to know each other all over again."

"But that's good," Ellie said with a laugh. "Since the two people you were couldn't exactly make a marriage work before." She patted Liz's hand. "Trust me. Needing to get to know each other all over again is a good thing."

"The only thing we have in common is sex."

Ellie laughed. Then she said, "And A Friend Indeed. He's really involved and he wants to stay involved."

"Yeah, but I think he only went to work for A Friend Indeed to get to me."

"At first, maybe. But I watched him last night. He was sincere in getting to know our people. He's actually mentoring Billy. He's volunteered to do more work. This guy is in for the long haul."

Until the first crisis with his own company came along. Until a business acquaintance was more important than Billy. Until she was back in his bed and he considered that to be enough time spent with her.

She squeezed her eyes shut. There were just too many variables.

Cain called her every day, and every day she phoned Ava. "He's coming home on Friday morning," she told Ava the following Monday morning. "His dad is recovering well from the surgery, but he wants to stay the extra four days to be sure. His mother is calm. His sister is there for both of them."

The relief was evident in Ava's voice when she said, "That's great." She paused then asked, "Did he say if he's coming to work on Friday?"

"He didn't say."

"I'll have things ready just in case."

"Great."

"Great."

There was an awkward silence before Liz said, "Goodbye, then."

But instead of saying goodbye, Ava said, "He doesn't really turn to people, you know?"

Not quite sure what Ava was driving at, Liz said simply, "I know."

"So it's kind of significant that he turned to you."

Liz swallowed. Now she understood. The fact that Cain had Liz touch base with his PA for him proved that Cain and Liz had a connection. Ava was probing and hinting right now because she didn't want to see Cain hurt.

"I'll call you if he calls again," Liz said lightly,

trying to get off the phone without the serious discussion Ava wanted to have. Then she said goodbye, hung up the phone and put her head in her hands.

No one knew better than Liz that it was significant that Cain had reached out to her. But she couldn't just jump off the deep end and let herself fall head over heels in love. She had to be careful. She had to be smart. Somehow or other *he* had to prove that if she let herself fall in love with him, things really would be different this time.

Cain called Liz with a glowing report of his dad's prognosis when he returned on Friday. It was already noon, so she'd long ago finished cleaning his house and was on to her second house of the day. He'd asked her to come over, but Friday was the one day that she had an entire eight hours' worth of houses to clean. She begged off and he accepted her refusal easily, saying he was going to take a dip in his pool before he checked in with Ava.

"I'll see you tomorrow morning, then."

"Fran Watson's house?"

"Yes. That's the house I talked about with Ayleen."

She hadn't thought he'd jump into A Friend Indeed work so quickly, except she knew the physical activity relaxed him. So the next morning she woke early, put on her jeans and tank top and headed for Fran Watson's house.

Because the entire house needed new floors, Liz expected to see rolls of discounted carpeting and padding extending from the back of Cain's truck when she pulled into the driveway. At the very most, inexpensive tile or linoleum. Instead, she found Cain and Billy unloading boxes of oak flooring.

"Oh, Cain! This is too much."

"Not really." He heaved a box out of the truck. Though Liz tried not to look, she couldn't help herself. His muscles shifted and moved beneath his T-shirt, reminding her of times they'd played volleyball by the ocean, laughing, having a good time.

She turned away. She had to stop noticing

things, remembering things and begin to look in earnest for some kind of proof that these changes in him were permanent. That he wouldn't hurt her or desert her after he married her. That he really wanted a second chance.

He headed for the kitchen where he and Billy began stacking boxes of flooring. When he returned outside, he wiped sweat off his neck with a red handkerchief.

Expecting him to say something about his dad or to be uncomfortable about the fact that the last time they'd seen each other, he'd kissed her, Liz was surprised when he said, "I got the hardwood at a discount supply store."

She almost couldn't believe this was the same man who had called her every day with reports on his dad, the guy who'd wanted to spend Friday afternoon with her. He seemed so distant, so cool.

Of course, they were working—and Billy was only a few feet away in the kitchen.

"Enough for the whole house?"

"I'm going to do the kitchen in a tile of some sort. If you've got kids in a kitchen, it's best to stay away from wood. Then I'm putting carpet in the bedrooms." He caught her gaze. "Personally, I like the soft feeling of carpet when I first roll out of bed."

Unwanted memories surfaced again. He'd always loved soft carpet, soft towels, soft pajamas. Especially hers. He'd said that was part of why he liked her. She didn't just wear soft clothes. *She* was incredibly soft. The softest woman he'd ever held. Even years later, she could remember the warmth of happiness from his compliment. And a glance in Cain's eyes told her that was why he'd said it.

Billy walked by with a box of wood on his shoulder. "I think we should listen to him. He's pretty smart."

Cain winced at the praise, but Liz laughed, grateful Billy had brought them back where they belonged.

When the kitchen door closed behind Billy, she turned to Cain. "I think he's officially your number-one fan."

"I just don't want him to be too big of a fan.

One mistake and I can undo every good thing we've accomplished by being friends."

"Just keep teaching him and you'll be fine." She glanced in the back of the truck, at the stacks of boxes of wood and the table saw. "What am I going to do?"

"I pretty much figure you'll be our cutter."

She studied the wicked-looking blade on the table saw then gaped at him. "I'm going to use *that?*"

"I need Billy's strength for the rubber mallet. I'm going to be the one on the nail gun. That leaves the saw for you."

"Oh, good grief!"

"You can do it. It's not nearly as complicated as it looks."

As it turned out, most of the morning was spent ripping out the old flooring in their target rooms, and carting it to the Dumpster Cain had arranged to have in Fran's backyard. He'd brought safety glasses, gloves and all the equipment they'd need, plus lunch, because Fran also didn't want to be in the house while they worked.

"How did you have the time to get all this together?"

"I didn't stay at work yesterday. I handled the important messages, then told Ava to arrange for the lunch and the things we'd need like safety glasses, then I headed to the building supply store."

"You did this yesterday?"

"Yes."

She wanted to ask, "After spending an entire week out of the office, you weren't clamoring to get back to work?" But she didn't. His actions spoke louder than any words he could have said.

When they began installing the new floors, Liz did some of the cutting, but Billy did his share, too. He'd paid attention as Cain showed Liz how to use the saw and easily stepped into the role. He and Cain worked like a team that had been together for decades, not a few weeks, and Liz marveled at their connection. She marveled at Cain's easy patience with the boy, and even the way he tempered his reactions to her around Billy.

There was no mention of the kiss. No mention

of the way he'd called her for support. But there was something about the way he looked at her that said more than words could that his feelings for her had grown, sharpened. When their hands accidentally brushed, he would let his fingers linger, as if he wanted the contact but knew it wasn't the place or time.

At the end of the day, he and Billy gathered the saw and tools for installing the floors and stowed them in his truck. "One more day and the hardwood's in. Next week we lay carpet. The week after, we get the linoleum in the kitchen. Piece of cake."

As he said all that, he punched notes into his BlackBerry. Probably a summary for Ayleen of what they'd accomplished that day.

He jumped into the truck. On the passenger's side, Billy followed suit. With a flick of a key, his truck's engine roared to life.

Liz stepped back, out of his way, then she ambled to her car and slid inside. When Cain's truck rolled out of the driveway and into the street, she laid her head on her steering wheel in dismay.

She finally understood why he hadn't made a big deal out of calling her or even out of kissing her the night of Joni's barbecue. This life they were building had become normal to him. Working with her on the Friend Indeed houses, mentoring Billy, calling her to talk about his family, even kissing her had become routine for him. He was different, eased into an entirely different way to live, and he was easing her in, too. And the next time they were alone she had no doubt he'd suggest a reconciliation.

She lifted her head and started her car. She hadn't forgotten that she had something she needed to tell him. She'd been waiting for the right time. But she finally saw the right time wasn't going to magically materialize. And even if it did, he might take hold of the conversation and she'd lose the chance to tell him about their baby.

She had to visit him, at home, and get the final piece of their past out in the open.

CHAPTER TEN

MONDAY MORNING, when Ava paged Cain on the intercom to tell him he had a call from Liz, he dropped to his desk chair and grabbed the phone. "Liz?"

"You know your assistant hates me, right?"

"Ava? She doesn't hate anybody." He paused. "But I'm glad you called."

She sighed. "You don't even know why I'm calling."

He was hoping that she'd missed him. Hoping she wanted to see him outside of work or A Friend Indeed. He'd settle for her simply wanting to talk to him. "I'm hoping you wanted to talk to me."

"I do. But privately. Would you have a few minutes to see me tonight?"

Privately? He fell back in his chair in disbelief. Then he scrambled up again. "Sure."

"I'll be over around six. Right after work."

"Great."

He hung up the phone. "Ava! I'm going to need a bottle of champagne and some fresh flowers for the house."

She walked to his office door and leaned against the jamb. "And why would you need that?"

"I'm having a guest tonight."

Her eyes narrowed. "The Happy Maids woman?"

Ah. So Liz wasn't so far off the mark after all. Ava didn't like her. "Am I sensing a bit of a problem?"

"Cain, you're a rich guy. You don't like little people, remember? It amazed me that you were working for A Friend Indeed, then I remembered how pretty Liz Harper is."

"Why do you care?"

"I worry about you because you're doing so many things out of character lately that you're scaring me." Sounding very much like his mother, she pushed away from the doorjamb and came into the room. "How do you know she's not after your money?"

"Because she refused alimony when we divorced."

Ava looked aghast. "She's your ex-wife."

"I probably should have told you that before this."

Ava studied him with narrowed eyes. "Getting involved with an ex is never a good idea."

He forced his attention back to the work on his desk. "I don't want to get involved with my ex." He *didn't* want to get involved with his *ex*. The old relationship hadn't worked. He wanted something new. Something better. He wanted something with the new Liz.

"Then why the champagne and flowers?"

Trying to ignore her, he tapped his pen on his desk. He and Ava had never really had a personal conversation. Even though she'd handled every nitpicky need in his life and knew him as much as anybody could, she'd kept the line of propriety with him. He couldn't believe she was walking over it now.

She took a few more steps into the room. "Cain, I know you well enough to know that you're up to something. Why not just tell me? Maybe I can help?"

Help? He wasn't the kind of man to confide about things like relationships with anyone let alone someone he worked with. But he'd ruined his marriage by being clueless. And right now he might be making progress with Liz, but he knew one wrong word could ruin everything.

Maybe he could use some help?

He *did* trust Ava. Plus, he would do anything, even ask for help, to figure out the best way to start over again with Liz.

"I don't want to get involved with my ex-wife because I want us to start over again."

"There's a difference?"

"Liz is different." He leaned back in his chair and tossed his pen to his desk. "I'm very different. I want our relationship to be different."

Ava walked closer to the desk. "You're serious."

"Never more serious. She's the only woman I've ever really loved. Our marriage got screwed up when my brother died." He wouldn't tell her the whole story. Just enough that she'd understand

Liz wasn't at fault in their bad marriage. "I withdrew and I basically left her alone. I wasn't surprised when she left. She's one of the most kind, most honest, most wonderful people I've ever met. Another woman would have been gone after six months. She stayed three long years. And I hurt her." He pulled in a breath. "She shouldn't want me back."

"But you think she does?"

"I think she still loves me."

"Wow."

"So now I want her back and I have no idea how to go about getting her back."

"You're sure this is the right thing?"

"Absolutely."

"You're not going to hurt her again?"

Cain laughed. Leave it to Ava to so quickly take Liz's side now that she knew Cain had been at fault.

"I swear."

"Okay, then for starters, I wouldn't do the things you did the last time around."

"That's the problem. The last time I wined and

dined her. Swept her off her feet." He half smiled at the memory. "If I don't wine and dine her—" He caught Ava's gaze. "How is she going to know I'm interested?"

"Lots of ways. But you don't want to use champagne and flowers. That would be too much like the past. Plus she's a businesswoman now." Her face scrunched as she thought for a second, then she said, "What time is she coming?"

"Six. Right after work."

"Feed her dinner." She sat on the seat in front of Cain's desk. "Trust a working woman on this one. Be practical."

"I've spent the past few weeks being practical. Pretending we were work buddies at A Friend Indeed." He wouldn't mention the kiss after the barbecue. The sweet memory might linger in his mind, but spending the following two weeks in Kansas had wiped away any opportunity he might have had to talk about it or expand on it with Liz. When he returned home, they'd had to pretend to be just friends in front of Billy. Private time was at a premium and he didn't want to waste it.

"This might be my only chance to be romantic."

"I didn't say you couldn't be romantic. I just said be practical first. Feed her. Have a normal conversation. Then do whatever it is you want to do romantically."

Cain's mouth twisted with a chagrined smile. What he wanted to do and what he had finally figured out was appropriate for a first date were two totally different things. Still, this might be his only shot. He had to play by the rules.

"All right. I'll try it your way."

Ava rose. "We should talk more often. Makes me feel like you're almost human."

He laughed. "Trust me. I'm fully human." Otherwise, Liz wouldn't have been able to break his heart the last time around. He also wouldn't be worried that she could very well break it this time, too.

At a quarter to six that night, with steaks sizzling on the grill and his refrigerator stocked with beer,

Ava's words repeated themselves in Cain's head. The first time around he'd done his damnedest to impress Liz. He hadn't been practical at all. His head had been in the clouds. This time around he would be better, smarter.

The doorbell sounded just as the steaks were ready to come off the grill. He raced through his downstairs, opened the door and pulled her inside. "Steaks have to come off the grill. Follow me."

"I didn't want you to cook dinner!"

"I like to grill." He did and she knew that, so that eased them past hurdle one.

She followed him through the downstairs into the kitchen and toward the French doors to the patio. "I still didn't want you to cook for me. I can't stay that long."

"You can stay long enough to eat one measly steak."

He said the words stepping out onto the cool stone floor of his patio.

Liz paused on the threshold. "This is beautiful."

He glanced around at the yellow chaise lounges,

the sunlight glistening off the blue water in the huge pool and the big umbrella table with the white linen tablecloth rustling in the breeze coming off the water just past his backyard. He hardly noticed how nice it was. With the exception of grilling and sometimes using the pool, he was never out here. In the past six years, he hadn't merely worked too much, he missed too much. He didn't enjoy what he had. Or the people in his life.

Maybe that's what Ava meant when she told him to be practical. To be normal.

"There's beer in the fridge."

She stopped midstep. "Beer?"

"Yes. Get me one and one for yourself, while I get these steaks off."

"Sure."

By the time she returned, he had the steaks on two plates, along with foil-wrapped potatoes and veggies, both of which he'd also cooked on the grill.

Studying the food he'd prepared, she handed him a beer. "This looks great."

He shrugged and motioned for her to take a seat. "All easy to do on a grill."

"I'm impressed."

He sat across from her. "I don't want you to be impressed. I want you to eat."

She unwrapped her potato and reached for the butter and sour cream. "I think you really were serious about seeing me put on some weight."

He laughed. "I like you just the way you are." His compliment didn't surprise him as it popped out of his mouth. Ava wanted him to behave normally, which he took to mean behave as his real self, and that was how he felt. But the compliment embarrassed Liz. Her cheeks reddened endearingly.

He wanted to tell her how beautiful she was but Ava's words rang in his head again. *Be practical.* He hadn't been practical the first time and as a result they'd never gotten to know each other. They'd each married a stranger.

"So tell me about your family."

She peeked up at him. "I did, remember?"

"You told me about your dad…about your past.

I'm interested in your family now. You said you had sisters."

She licked her lips, stalling, obviously thinking about whether or not she should speak, what she should say, if she should say anything at all. Cain's heart nearly stopped. This was it, the big test of whether or not she was interested in a real relationship, and she was hesitating over the easy questions.

Could he have read this whole situation wrong? The kiss before he left for Kansas? The lifeline she'd been while his father was sick? The heated looks and lingering touches at the Friend Indeed houses?

"My mom works as a nurse."

Relief poured through him. "No kidding?" Feigning nonchalance he didn't feel, he unwrapped the foil around his veggies. He had to be comfortable if he wanted her to be comfortable. "What about your sisters? What do they do?"

"My older sister is a physician's assistant. My younger sister is a pharmaceutical sales rep."

"Interesting. Everybody's in medicine in some way." He took a bite of broccoli.

Liz cut a strip off her steak. "Except me."

"You're still helping people."

"Yeah, but my degree's in business. I didn't get the nerves of steel my mother had. I couldn't have gone into medicine. I'm the family rebel."

"Me, too. My dad owned a chain of hardware stores. And here I am in Miami, running three companies that use hardware but aren't in the hardware business."

"I always wondered why you didn't just stay in Kansas and join the family business."

"When it was time for me to go to school, the stores hit a rough patch. That's why I put myself through university." He shook his head. "But what a backhanded lucky break. It led me to the work I love."

"You *were* lucky."

The second the words were out of her mouth, Liz regretted them. Cain might have been lucky in business but he hadn't been lucky in life. He'd suffered a horrible tragedy in the loss of his brother, particularly since he'd been the driver of the car. Their marriage had failed. Now she was here to tell him of another heartbreak. The conversation had been going in the absolute right direction until she'd made her stupid comment about him being lucky.

"I was lucky, but not entirely. Once I figured out what I wanted to do with my life I had to work hard to make it happen."

She nearly breathed a sigh of relief that he hadn't taken her comment the wrong way and challenged it as he could have. "True."

He slid his hand across the table. "And that's why I'm glad you wanted to talk tonight." He pulled in a breath, reached for her fingers. Before Liz could stop him he had his hand wrapped around hers. "I know I'm going to say this badly, but I can't go on the way we have been over the past few weeks." He caught her stunned gaze. "I don't want a reconciliation. Neither one of us wants to go back to what we had." He brought her fingers to his lips and kissed them. "But there's no law that says we can't start over. We're both different—"

Liz's breath froze in her lungs. She was too late! She loved him and now he was falling for her. She'd thought she'd fallen first and maybe too fast because Cain was so different that it was easy for her to see that and respond to it. But he was right with her. Falling as fast and as hard as she had been. Now she had to scramble to set things right.

Only with effort did she find the air and ability to speak. "Oh, Cain, we can't pretend we don't have a past."

"Sure we can."

"We can't!" She sucked in a breath, calmed herself. For weeks she'd been waiting for the right time to tell him her secret. She'd hesitated when she should have simply been brave and told him. She couldn't let another opportunity pass. "Cain, I can't forget the past and neither can you. We have to deal with it. I left you because I had a miscarriage. I needed help. Real help to get beyond it."

His face shifted from happy to shocked. "You were pregnant?"

"Yes."

"And you didn't tell me?" He let go of her hand and combed his fingers through his hair.

"I *couldn't* tell you—"

Music suddenly poured from Liz's cell phone. She pulled it from her jeans pocket, hoping that a glance at caller ID would allow her to ignore it. When she saw it was Ayleen, she almost groaned. She couldn't ignore a call from A Friend Indeed.

She glanced at Cain in apology, but opened her phone and answered. "Hey, Ayleen. What's up?"

"We got an emergency call tonight. Is the old Rogerson place clean?"

An emergency meant a woman had suddenly run from her husband or boyfriend. She could be hurt. Mentally and physically. She could have kids with her.

Liz sat up, coming to attention, breaking eye contact with Cain. "Yes. It's ready."

Ayleen breathed a sigh of relief. "Great. Can you be there to meet the family?"

"Absolutely." Once again, she didn't hesitate but she caught Cain's gaze. "I can be there in a half an hour."

"No rush. The family's in transit. Their estimated arrival time is forty minutes."

"Ten minutes to spare." Ten minutes to talk Cain through this. "I'll call you later, after they're settled." She snapped her phone closed. Her gaze still clinging to Cain's, she said, "I'm sorry."

"For a miscarriage that wasn't your fault? For not telling me you were pregnant? Or for leaving me now before I can even wrap my head around it?"

"For all three."

He rubbed his hand across the back of his neck, and turned away. Fear trickled down her spine. Not for herself, for him. She didn't want him to blame himself. Or be angry with himself.

"I know you have questions. I'm not sure I can answer them all, but I'll try."

He faced her again. "You know what? I get it." He shrugged. "We were both in a bad place. You did what you had to do. I'm stunned about losing a baby, but I can deal with that."

Her phone rang. She longed to ignore it, but knew what happened when A Friend Indeed was in crisis mode. The troops rallied. They called each other, making arrangements for what each would do. She couldn't ignore a call.

She flipped open her phone. "Hello."

"It's me, Ellie. Who's getting the groceries for the Rogerson house? You or me?"

"Could you do it?"

"Sure. See you, boss."

Warring needs tore her apart as she closed her phone. She wanted to be here for Cain, but he seemed to be handling this well. Three years had passed. Though she was sure he'd mourn the loss, it wasn't the same as actually going through it.

And the woman racing to the Friend Indeed house needed her. This was what she was trained to do.

Before she could speak, Cain did. "Go. I'm fine."

Liz studied his face and he smiled weakly. "Seriously, I'm fine. I'll call you."

His smile, though shaky, reassured her.

She rose. Her voice carried a gentle warning when she said, "If you don't call me, I'm calling you."

He smiled again. This time stronger. "Okay."

She turned and walked back into the house, through the downstairs and to the front door. On her way to her car she stopped and glanced back.

He'd taken that so well that maybe, just maybe, they really could have the new beginning he wanted.

CHAPTER ELEVEN

WALKING INTO THE shower the following Saturday, Cain cursed himself. He'd hardly slept since Monday night, and, when he had, he'd dreamed about things that made him crazy. The smoothness of Liz's perfect pink skin. The way her green eyes smoldered with need in the throes of passion. The feeling of her teeth scraping along his chest.

He shouldn't want her. *Shouldn't.* He was smarter than to want somebody who didn't want him.

She'd been so hesitant about spending time with him, to befriend him, to even consider anything romantic between them, yet he'd been oblivious to what her behavior was telling him. Just as he had been in their marriage. Now that he knew the real reason she'd left him, her not wanting anything to do with him made perfect sense.

He ducked his head under the spray, trying to rid himself of the overwhelming shame that wanted to strangle him, but he couldn't. After his three years of guilt over his brother's death, he knew he couldn't assume responsibility for something that had been out of his control. And if her secret had simply been a matter of a miscarriage, he probably could have absolved himself. But how could he forgive himself for being so self-absorbed that his wife couldn't tell him she was pregnant? How could he forgive himself when her telling him about their baby might have been the thing that brought him back to life, bridged their marital gap, kept them together?

Stepping out of the shower, he grabbed a towel, telling himself to stop thinking about it. Running it over and over and over in his head wouldn't change anything. But memories of those final few months together had taken on new meaning and they haunted him.

And he could not—he would not—forgive himself.

* * *

At Amanda's house, Cain told Billy to take his time, hoping to delay seeing Liz. He hadn't called her as he told her he would but she also hadn't called him. He suspected she'd been busy with the new family moving into the Friend Indeed house. And for that he was grateful. He'd wanted to be alone. He didn't want to talk this out with her. Worse, he didn't want her to tell him it was "okay" that he hadn't been there for her. It wasn't "okay." It was abysmal—sinful—that he'd been so oblivious that his wife had to suffer in silence.

But the bad thing about avoiding her all week was that Billy would now witness their first meeting since she told him about their baby.

He pulled his truck into Fran's empty driveway. "No Liz," he mumbled, hardly realizing he was talking.

Billy pushed open the truck door. "Isn't there some kind of big party tonight?"

Cain turned to Billy. "Yes." How could he have forgotten? "A Friend Indeed's fund-raiser." On top of the new family that had moved in on Monday night, Liz had probably been occupied all week with last-minute details for the ball.

Billy jumped out of the truck. "And she's the boss of the whole deal, right?"

Cain nodded.

"So she's not going to be here." Billy slammed his door closed.

Cain's entire body sagged with relief. Until he remembered that he'd see her that night at the ball—

Unless he didn't go.

All things considered, that might be the right thing to do. Not for himself, but for her. This was her big night. He didn't want to ruin it. And seeing him sure as hell could ruin it for her. He'd been a nightmare husband. And when they'd "met" again in his kitchen when she came to work as his maid, she hadn't wanted to be around him. Yet he'd forced himself back into her life. He couldn't even imagine the pressure she'd endured for the weeks they'd worked together, the weeks he'd insinuated himself into A Friend Indeed. Not going would be a kindness to her.

For the next eight hours, he kept himself busy so he didn't have to think about Liz or the fundraiser ball or their god-awful marriage. But at the end of the day he remembered that he'd promised Ayleen he would mingle with the guests, talking about the work he'd done, hoping to inspire other contractors and business owners to get involved in a more personal way. So if he didn't show, Ayleen would get upset and then Liz would worry about him.

He didn't want Liz to have to worry about him anymore. He wasn't her burden. He'd fulfill his responsibility and go to the ball, but he'd let her alone.

Liz had spent all day at the home of Mr. and Mrs. Leonard Brill, the couple who had volunteered their mansion for the ball for A Friend Indeed. After seeing to all the last-minute deliveries and details, she'd even dressed in one of their myriad spare bedrooms.

The event itself wasn't huge. Only a hundred people were attending. That was why the Brill mansion was the perfect choice. It was big enough to be luxurious, but not so large that the fundraiser lost its air of intimacy. But the ball didn't need to be immense. All the people invited were big contributors. Liz expected to beat last year's donations by a wide margin, especially with the new guests Cain invited.

Walking into the empty ballroom ten minutes before the guests were due to arrive, she pressed her hand to her stomach. *Cain.* Just thinking his name gave her butterflies. He hadn't called her as he had promised, but she'd been overwhelmed with the ball, the new family in the Rogerson house and Happy Maids. He probably knew that and didn't want to add any more stress to her week.

But she remembered the expression on his face when she left, the calm way he'd taken the explanation of why she'd ended their marriage, and she not only knew she'd done the right thing by telling him, she also knew they were going to be okay.

Maybe better than okay.

"You look fabulous!" Wearing a peach sequined gown Ayleen floated across the empty dance floor to Liz, who pirouetted in her red strapless gown.

"Wow." Ellie joined them. "You two are going to be the talk of the town."

Liz laughed at Ellie, who looked like a vision in her aqua halter-top gown, her blond hair spilling around her in a riot of curls. "I think *you're* going to be the talk of the town."

She laughed. "Maybe we should all just settle for making our special men drool."

"My husband's past drooling," Ayleen said with a laugh, but just as quickly she frowned and her eyes narrowed at Liz. "I know Ellie is dating that lifeguard, but I've heard nothing about a special man in *your* life."

Liz felt her face redden and suspected it was probably as bright as her dress.

"Oh, come on!" Ellie chided. "Tell her about Cain."

Ayleen's eyebrows rose. "Our Cain?"

Ellie leaned in conspiratorially. "He was Liz's Cain long before he was A Friend Indeed's. He's her ex."

Ayleen's mouth dropped open. "No kidding."

"And I have a feeling," Ellie singsonged, "that they're not going to be exes long."

"Is that true?" Ayleen asked, facing Liz.

Liz sighed. "I have no idea."

Ellie playfully slapped her forearm. "You need to be more confident. That man loves you. I can see it in his face."

"But we have issues."

"Oh, pish posh!" Ayleen said. "Do you love him?"

"I don't ever think I ever stopped." As the words came out of her mouth, Liz realized how true they were. That was why she'd been so afraid to tell him about the miscarriage. She didn't want to hurt him or lose him. Which is why she was so grateful he'd reacted as well as he had to the news. She loved him. She always had and now that her secret had been confessed, they could finally move on with their lives.

"Then trust our magic friend. If she says he loves you, he loves you." She patted her hand. "You need to relax."

Cain strode up the stone sidewalk to the elaborate entrance of the Brill mansion. Twin fountains on both sides of the walk were lit by blue-and-gold lights. At the top of ten wide stone steps, columns welcomed guests to a cut-glass front door.

He could see why A Friend Indeed had chosen the Brill residence for their ball. It was one of Miami's most beautiful mansions. Plus, it was small enough to create an intimate atmosphere for guests. The kind of atmosphere that would allow Ayleen to personally walk among the guests and gather checks. Cain himself had an obscenely large check in his pocket. He wanted Liz to succeed.

Liz.

He could picture her now, excited about being

pregnant and not being able to tell him. Then devastated by the loss and not being able to depend on him.

He cursed himself in his head for remembering, just as Leonard opened the front door.

"Cain! Welcome."

Cain pasted on a smile and stepped into the foyer. "Good evening, Mr. Brill."

"Call me Leonard, please," the older, gray-haired gentleman said as he directed Cain to the right. "Everyone's in the ballroom."

Nerves jangled through Cain as he entered the grand room. His eyes instantly scanned the crowd milling around the room, looking at artwork that had been donated for a silent auction that was also part of the event. A string quartet played in a corner as a dance band set up across the room.

He didn't see Liz, but he knew she was here and his heart began to hammer in anticipation. He shook his head. He had to get over this. Let her go. Let her find somebody worthy of her love.

Plus, he had a job at this fund-raiser. Ayleen had assigned him the task of walking around, talking about what he'd done for the houses so he could generate support and bigger contributions.

But only ten minutes into a conversation with a potential contributor he spotted Liz. As he spoke to Brad Coleman, his eyes had been surreptitiously scanning the room and he saw her standing with a small group of women, engaged in lively conversation.

He'd missed seeing her before because her beautiful black hair wasn't cascading over her shoulders, in a bouncy ponytail or even pulled back into a Happy Maids bun. It had been swept up into an elegant hairdo that gave her the look of a princess or aristocrat.

He let his eyes move lower and his breath whooshed from his lungs. Her dress was red—strapless—and didn't so much cling to her curves as gently caress them. He swallowed hard just as she turned and noticed him. She smiled hesitantly and his heart swelled with something that felt very much like love. But he stopped that, too.

He didn't deserve her. He never had.

"Why didn't you tell me that you and Liz had been married?"

Cain spun around and saw that Brad had deserted him and Ayleen had taken his place.

"It didn't seem relevant."

She laughed. "Men. You never know what's relevant."

Since he was the one so distant his own wife couldn't tell him she was pregnant, Cain couldn't argue that.

"She looks very beautiful tonight, doesn't she?"

Cain's gaze followed the direction of Ayleen's. Taking in the way her gown clung to her curves, and the sparkle in her brilliant green eyes, his blood raced in his veins, but his chest tightened in sadness. He had to walk away from her. Give her a chance for a real life.

"Yes. She is beautiful."

"You should ask her to dance."

"I don't think so. In fact," he said, reaching into

his jacket pocket and producing his check, "I'll just give this to you."

Ayleen glanced at the check, then up at him. "This is the second time you've tried to give A Friend Indeed a check without going through the proper channels."

"I thought you were the proper channel."

"And I thought you'd want to give it to your ex-wife, so she could be impressed and proud of you."

He reared back as if she'd physically slapped him. If there were two things Liz should never be of him, they were proud or impressed.

He pressed the check into Ayleen's hand. "You take it."

She studied his face. "So you don't have to speak with her?" She smiled ruefully. "Cain, this is wrong. She's excited to see you tonight and you're running?"

"Believe me. This is for her benefit, not mine." He lifted his eyes and luckily saw one of the guests he'd had Ayleen invite. "And before you ask why, I see one of my contributors." He slid away. "I'll see you later."

Liz shifted through the crowd, pausing to speak with people, asking if there was anything anyone needed, wishing everyone a good time. The dance band had been playing for about an hour. Dancers swayed and gyrated around the room. The silent auction proceeded as planned. Still, she walked around, introduced herself, saw to every tiny detail.

After another hour of pretending it didn't matter that Cain had ignored her when she'd smiled at him, she couldn't lie to herself anymore. He'd chosen not to speak with her. He hadn't said hello. Hadn't even returned her smile.

Pulling in a breath, she greeted a passing couple who praised her for the beautiful ball. But questions about why Cain wouldn't talk to her raced through her head. What if Cain hadn't taken her news as well as he'd seemed to? What if he'd been pretending? Or what if he was angry with her for not telling him she was pregnant?

It could be any of those things or all of them. She longed to find him and simply ask him, but she had a job to do. As if to punctuate that thought, a woman caught her hand and asked her a question about the auction. An elderly gentleman handed her a check. She couldn't walk two feet without someone stopping her.

The band took a break and the auction results were announced by Ayleen, with Liz by her side on the small elevated platform that acted as a stage for the band.

"Those are our winners," Ayleen finally said, having given the final name on the list of those who'd won the bids. "You know where the checks go," she added with a laugh. "Thank you very much for your participation in this event. A Friend Indeed couldn't exist without you and on behalf of the women we've helped, I thank you."

The group broke into a quiet round of applause and after a reasonable time Ayleen raised her hand to stop them.

"I'd also like to thank Liz Harper for all of her

hard work, not just on this ball but also for the group on a daily basis."

The crowd applauded again.

When they were through, Ayleen said, "And special thanks to Cain Nestor. He's been renovating the houses. Donating both his time and the materials to make the homes of our women some of the prettiest houses in their neighborhoods."

The crowd erupted in spontaneous, thunderous applause, and Liz felt such a stirring of pride for Cain, tears came to her eyes. He never saw what a wonderful person he was. But she did. And she'd made another huge mistake with him. She should have told him about their baby sooner.

Lost in her thoughts, she wasn't prepared when Ayleen caught her hand and pulled her forward, toward the microphone again.

"What most of you don't know though is that Liz has been helping Cain. At first she acted as A Friend Indeed's liaison, but then she picked up a paintbrush and threw herself into the work, too. Cain and Liz are an unbeatable team."

She hugged Liz in thanks then turned away,

scanning the room. "Cain? Where are you? How about if you and Liz get the next set of the dancing started, so everyone can see who you are?"

Liz's mouth fell open in dismay. Ayleen had probably noticed Cain hadn't even spoken to her and was playing matchmaker. She didn't know Cain was upset about their child and he didn't want to talk with her. Liz had only figured it out herself. But there was nothing she could do to get out of this without embarrassing herself or Cain.

With her heart hammering in her chest, Liz looked down off the makeshift stage and searched the crowd for Cain. She found him in the back in a corner, watching her. Their gazes locked. She waited for him to look away. He didn't. She told herself to look away and couldn't. He walked out of the crowd to her.

Cain swallowed the last of the champagne in his glass and dropped it on the tray of a passing waiter. He wouldn't embarrass Liz by publicly refusing to dance with her. But he also knew this was as good of a time as any to get their relationship on track. She didn't want a second chance with him. He didn't deserve one. But they both worked for A Friend Indeed. So they had to spend time together. They couldn't ignore each other forever.

The whole room stilled as he and Liz met in the center of the dance floor. He pulled her into his arms, and the band began to play a waltz. Forcing himself to focus on the music, he tried to ignore her sweet scent, but it swirled around them like the notes of the song, tempting him. Especially when she melted against him. Not in surrender, but in acknowledgment. They would always have chemistry. But sometimes that wasn't enough.

He wasn't enough. She was worthy of someone much, much better.

The music vibrated around them as other dancers eased onto the floor. In minutes they were surrounded by a happy crowd. Not the center of attention, anymore. Not even on anyone's radar. He could slip away.

Just as he was ready to excuse himself and end

the dance, she pulled back. Her shiny green eyes searched his.

"Are you okay?"

"I'm fine." He said the words casually then twirled her around to emphasize his lightness. He'd never make her feel responsible for him again.

She pulled back again. "But you're angry with me."

He laughed. "No, Liz. If there's one thing I'm not, it's angry with you."

"You have every right to be. I should have told you about our baby sooner."

The hurt in her voice skipped across his nerves like shards of glass. As if it wasn't bad enough he had to walk away from her, she was taking it all wrong.

"And I'm sorry. I'm very, very sorry."

He nearly squeezed his eyes shut in misery. He was the one who hadn't been there for her. Yet she was apologizing to him?

He stopped dancing, tugged his hand away from hers. "Stop."

"No. You told me on Monday night that you wanted to start over. I think we could—"

Other dancers nearly bumped into them. He caught her by the waist and hauled her against him, spinning them into the crowd again. "Don't say it," he said, nearly breathless from her nearness. They couldn't go on like this. And he'd made it worse by mentioning starting over before he knew just how bad he'd been as a husband. Now, in her innate fairness, or maybe because she was so kind, she was willing to try again. But he couldn't do that to her.

And if the only way to get her away from him, off the notion that somehow they belonged together, was to hurt her, then maybe one final hurt added to his long list of sins wouldn't matter.

"I made a mistake the other night when I mentioned reconciling. I was a lousy husband. You never should have married me. It's time we moved on. Time we let go. Time *you* let go."

With that he released her. The horrified expression on her face cut to his heart, but he ignored it, turned and walked off the dance floor. Letting her go was for the best. Even if it did break his heart.

Stunned, Liz turned and scanned the great room, until she found Ellie. She raced over. "I have to go."

Ellie's face fell. "What?"

"I'm sorry," she said, pulling Ellie with her as she ran through the foyer to the front door. "Everything's done, except the final goodbye and thank-you. Ayleen has already done the official thank-you. All you need to say is thank-you and good-night. Can you do that?"

Ellie said, "Sure, but—"

Liz didn't give her the chance to finish. She raced out the door and down the stone steps. The tinkling of the fountains followed her and the silver moon lit the way as she raced down the driveway to her car. The only thing missing from the scene was a pair of glass slippers.

Because like Cinderella, she'd lost her prince. Again.

The old Cain was back. And the worst of it was

Liz had brought him back. He'd pretended to take the news of their baby well, but the truth was he'd tumbled back into the horrible place where he'd lived the three years of their marriage. There had been no help for it. She couldn't have entered into a relationship with a secret hanging over them.

But she'd hurt him. More this time than she had by walking away from their marriage without a word.

He'd never forgive her.

She'd never forgive herself.

Balling up the skirt of her gown, she slid into her car and a horrible thought struck her. They had to work together in the morning. After the way he'd rejected her, dismissed her, she had to go to Fran's house in the morning and pretend nothing had happened.

CHAPTER TWELVE

THE NEXT MORNING, Cain nearly called Ayleen and begged off his work on Fran's house. He hadn't wanted to hurt Liz, but he'd had to to force her to get on with her life. So he didn't really want to spend eight hours with her, seeing her hurt, knowing he'd hurt her and knowing he really would spend the rest of his days without the one woman he wanted in his life. All because he could never see her needs. She might be right for him, but he most certainly wasn't right for her and he had to let her go.

But in the end he conceded that bailing on Fran's house wasn't the thing to do. He had made a commitment to A Friend Indeed. Fran shouldn't have to wait for her house to be finished because he and Liz shouldn't be working together.

He rolled his truck to a stop in front of Fran's

garage but didn't immediately open his truck door. Stuck in his thoughts, he stared at the empty space beside his truck.

"She'll be here," Billy said, undoubtedly assuming Cain was wondering where Liz was. "She never lets anybody down. Just ask my mom."

The kid's voice held the oddest note of both trust in Liz and scorn. It might have been simple teenage angst or it could have been that something had happened that morning to make him angry. Cain couldn't tell. Sooner or later, he'd get it out of him, but right now Cain's mind was still on Liz. About how his next step would have to be getting her off his work crew.

He shoved his truck door open and jumped out just as her little green car chugged into the driveway. He rushed back to his truck bed and immediately reached for the cooler and picnic basket. Intense and primal, the desire rose in him to get away before the need to talk to her, to touch her, became a hungry beast he couldn't control. He would have done anything, given anything, if there would have been a way they could start over, but they couldn't. He wouldn't do that to her. He would not ruin her life a second time.

Stepping out of her car, Liz saw the picnic basket and smiled shakily. "You brought lunch again."

He almost groaned. Even sweet Liz shouldn't be able to forgive him for how he'd rejected her the night before. Yet, here she was trying to get along, giving him the damned benefit of the doubt.

"Yes. I brought lunch." He turned away, taking the cooler and stowing it in the garage before he hauled the picnic basket into the kitchen.

Following him, she said, "What are we doing today?"

"We're finishing the carpet in the bedrooms." And it wasn't a three-person job. He and Billy had handled it alone the day before. This was his out, his way to save her, his way to save himself from the misery of being within arm's distance of the woman he'd always loved, but never deserved.

He faced her. "This is actually a two-person

job. Billy and I can handle it. I know you're probably tired from all the work you did for the ball yesterday." Casually, as if nothing were wrong, he leaned against the counter. "So why don't you go on home?"

She took a step back. "You want me to leave?"

"Yes." The wounded look in her eyes made him long to tell her he was sorry that he hadn't been there for her. To tell her how much he wished he could make all his misdeeds up to her. To tell her he wished there was a way they didn't have to give up on their relationship.

But he couldn't do that. The only honorable thing for him to do would be to sacrifice his own needs, so that she'd find someone who really would love her.

She stared at him, as if waiting for him to change his mind. As the clock above the sink ticked off the seconds, her eyes filled with tears. Without a word, she turned and raced out the door before Cain could even say goodbye.

Billy shook his head in wonder. "Are you nuts?"

Before he could stop himself, Cain said, "Trust me. This is for her own good."

It might have been for her good, but the sadness that shivered through him told Cain that he wouldn't ever get over this. Forcing her to find a better man was the best thing for her, but it was the worst that could happen to him.

In her office that morning and afternoon, Liz kept herself so busy catching up on the work she'd ignored while she worked on the ball that she didn't have time to think about Cain.

She knew telling him about their lost baby had caused him to close himself off. But this time he didn't seem to be closing himself off from the world. Only from her.

She refused to let herself think about any of it, and instead worked diligently in her office until it was dark. Then she walked to her car, head high, breaths deep and strong. She'd lost him twice now. But this time she'd lost him honestly. She'd lost him because she wouldn't start a relationship while hiding a secret. She'd done the right thing. She'd simply gotten the wrong result.

And now she would deal with it.

In her condo, she tossed her keys to the table by the door and reached for the hem of her T-shirt as she walked back to the shower. She might have lost him honestly but she'd still lost him, and it hurt so much even the soothing spray of her shower didn't help. She'd lost Cain's love, the affection she craved from him, but more than that she would have to live with the knowledge that he would torment himself for the rest of his life.

She knew he was a good man. If only he could forgive himself and live life in the now, he could be free. But he couldn't, not even for her. Not even for *them*.

After her shower, she wrapped herself in a robe and headed out to the kitchen to make herself some cocoa. She reached into the cupboard for a mug just as her cell phone rang. For the second time in as many weeks, she wished she could ignore it. She wanted to weep, not for herself but for Cain. For as much as it hurt her to lose him, she knew he suffered the torment of the damned. He'd never be happy.

But as an integral part of a charity that didn't sleep, she couldn't ignore any call. She reached over and picked up her phone. Seeing that the caller was Amanda, she said, "Hey, Amanda. What's up?"

"Liz! Liz! Billy is gone!"

"What do you mean gone?"

"We had a fight this morning that we didn't get to finish because Cain came to get him for work. When he got home this afternoon he tried to act as if nothing happened, but I picked up right where we left off." Amanda burst into tears. "I'm so sorry. I was so stupid. But I'm so afraid he'll turn out like his dad that I go overboard. And now he's gone. He just walked out, slamming the door. Before I could go after him he was gone. I didn't even see if he turned right or left. It was like he disappeared." She took a shuddering breath. "I've looked everywhere I know to look. He's nowhere."

Liz's own breath stuttered in her chest. Fear

for Billy overwhelmed her. "Don't worry. We'll find him."

"How? I've looked everywhere. And it's too soon to call the police. They make you wait twenty-four hours." She made a gurgling sound in her throat. "By the time twenty-four hours pass, anything could happen!"

"Okay, I'm calling Cain—" She made the offer without thinking. Even Amanda was surprised.

"Cain?"

"They talk a lot as they're working, Amanda. There's a good chance he'll know where Billy is."

Amanda breathed a sigh of relief. "Okay."

But Liz's breath froze when she realized what she'd done. Now she had to call Cain. "You sit tight. I'll call you back as soon as I talk to him."

"Okay."

Liz clicked off and immediately dialed Cain's cell phone. She wouldn't let herself think about the fact that he hated her now. Wouldn't let herself consider that he might ignore her plea for help.

"Liz?"

Relieved that he'd answered, Liz leaned against her counter and said simply, "Billy's gone."

"Gone?"

"He had a fight with Amanda. She says she knows she pushed a bit too hard, and he flew out of the house and was gone before she could even see what direction he ran in."

A few seconds passed in silence before Cain said, "Look, Liz, I'm going to be honest. I think I know where Billy is, but you can't come with me."

"Like hell I can't!" He might have been able to kick her off the job site that morning, but Billy was her responsibility, and she wasn't letting Cain push her out of finding him.

"I think he's gone to his father's. If he has, this could be dangerous."

"I get that. But I'm trained for this! *You* aren't. If either one of us goes, it should be me."

There was a long pause. Finally Cain blew his breath out on a sigh. "I can't let you go alone, so we have to go together. Be ready when I get to your apartment." He stopped. "Where is your apartment?"

She gave him the address and, as he clicked off, she raced into her bedroom and pulled on jeans and a tank top. By the time he arrived in front of her building, she was already on the sidewalk.

She jumped into his Porsche and he raced away. The humid Miami air swirled around her as they roared down the street. With Cain's attention on driving, Liz glanced around at the car she'd loved when they were married. Memories of driving down this very highway in this very car, six years ago, before all their troubles, assailed her. They were so sweet and so poignant that part of her longed to pretend that everything was okay between them.

But that was their biggest problem. When things weren't working out, they'd tried to pretend they were. She was done with that and Cain was, too. She had to accept that they were over.

Cain tried not to think about Liz sitting next to him as he drove to Billy's old house, the house

he and Amanda had lived in with an abusive father. He prayed that Billy hadn't been so angry
with his mom that he told his father the location
of their safe house. If they didn't get to Billy on
time, Billy's dad could be on his way to Amanda's before they could warn her.

He pressed his gas pedal to the floor. Billy's
dad lived far enough away that Billy would have
had to take a bus. Cain didn't know the schedule,
but he prayed Billy hadn't been lucky enough to
walk out onto the street and hop on a bus. If he'd
had to wait that bought him and Liz time to get to
him. So there was still hope. Slim hope. But hope.

Nearing Billy's old neighborhood, Cain also
prayed that if Billy had made it to his dad's and
had had the gumption to refuse to tell his dad
where his mom and sister were that his dad hadn't
taken his fists to him.

A sick feeling rose up in him. There were too
many ways this night could end badly.

Because he didn't have an exact address, Cain
slowed his car. When he did, he heard Liz suck
in a breath.

He automatically reached for her hand. "Don't worry. We'll do this."

The feeling of her hand in his brought an ache to his chest. He knew he shouldn't have touched her. But she looked so sad and he was so scared that it came automatically to him. She smiled at him across the console and his heart constricted. He'd give anything to deserve the trust she had in him.

He glanced away, at the area around them.

"Billy talked about a bar that was two buildings down from his house and going to the convenience store across the street." Cain let his Porsche roll along slowly as he and Liz scanned the area.

"There's the bar," Liz shouted, pointing. "And the convenience store."

"And Billy," Cain said, pointing at the kid sitting on the curb in front of a little blue house.

He found a parking space, and they pushed their way out of the car and raced up to Billy.

"Hey, Liz." Billy's eyes roved from Liz to Cain. "Hey, Cain."

"Hey." The kid's mood was sad more than upset, so Cain took a cue from him. Not caring about his gray trousers, he casually sat on the curb beside Billy. Liz sat on the other side. "Your mom is worried."

He snorted a laugh. "My mom is always worried."

"Looks like she's got good reason this time," Liz said, turning and gesturing at the house behind them. "Is that your old place?"

Billy nodded.

"Dad not home?"

"He might be. I don't know."

Cain sat back, letting Liz take the lead in the conversation. She was the one who had been trained for this.

"You didn't go in?"

"I sorta feel like I'm doing that cutting off my nose to spite my face thing my mom talks about."

Cain chuckled and Liz out-and-out laughed.

He could hear the relief in her voice. He felt it, too. Billy had run, but he couldn't take the final steps. He probably liked his new life. Even if his old life sometimes seemed like a way out of his troubles, he really didn't want to go back.

"Yeah. That's probably accurate." She waited a few seconds then said, "Do you want to talk about it?"

Billy shrugged. "Same old stuff."

"I'm not familiar with the stuff, so you'll have to fill me in."

"She's afraid of everything."

Liz's eyebrows rose. "She has good reason, Billy."

"I'm not my dad and I'm tired of paying for his mistakes."

Cain got a sudden inspiration and before Liz could reply, he said, "How does she make you pay?"

"She yells at me. I have a curfew."

"That's not paying for your dad's mistakes, Billy. That's her guiding you, looking out for your welfare, being a mom."

Billy looked at him sharply. "No one else I know has a curfew."

"Maybe that's why half your friends are in trouble." Cain sighed and shifted on the curb, glancing at Liz who only gave him a look with her eyes that encouraged him to continue.

"Look, trust isn't handed out like hall passes in school. You have to earn it."

Unexpectedly, he thought of Liz, of all the ways he'd failed her and yet she trusted him. She trusted him when he didn't trust himself. Liz had always believed in him. Even when he let her down, she believed he'd do the right thing the next time.

Hooking his thumb toward the house behind them, he said, "Earning trust isn't easy, but running back to the past isn't the alternative. It's just a way of staying right where you are. Never learning from your mistakes. Never having what you want." A strange feeling bubbled up in him as he said that. As if he wasn't talking to Billy but to himself.

He cleared his throat. "But that means you're going to have to do a thing or two to earn your mom's trust."

"Like what?"

"Like not arguing about the curfew and coming in on time. Like telling her where you're going." He gave Billy a friendly nudge with his shoulder. "Like getting your grades up in school."

Billy snorted a laugh.

"So it sounds as if you agree that there's room for improvement."

"I guess."

Cain clasped his hand on Billy's shoulder. "Let's get you back to your mom."

Billy rose. "Okay."

Liz rose, too.

"But first let's go across the street and get a gallon of ice cream. What kind does your mom like?"

Billy blinked. "Chocolate. Why?"

"It never hurts to bring a present when you've made a mistake."

* * *

When Liz, Cain and Billy walked in the kitchen door of Amanda's house, Amanda burst into tears.

Billy held out a brown bag to his mom. "I'm sorry, Mom. I shouldn't have been mad. I know all your rules are to protect me. I'll do better."

Amanda took the bag and set it on the table without looking at it so she could grab Billy in a hug. Sobbing out her fear, she clung to him and wept.

Liz caught Cain's gaze and motioned that they should leave. He hesitated, but she headed for the door and he followed her.

The strangest feelings assaulted him. By punishing himself for something so far in the past he couldn't change it, he wasn't moving on. And he also wasn't learning any lessons. He was losing the one thing he'd always wanted—Liz. She was never the one to condemn him. He continually condemned himself. What if she was correct. What if—for once in his life—he gave himself a break?

She stepped out onto the sidewalk, walked to the driveway and got into his car.

Their car.

He squeezed his eyes shut and pressed his lips together. She wanted to forgive him. Was it so wrong to want to forgive himself?

CHAPTER THIRTEEN

THE NEXT MORNING, Liz lay on her sofa, wrapped in a blanket, drinking hot cocoa, even though the temperature outside had long ago passed eighty.

She had awakened so sad and lonely, after a sleepless night, that she considered it a real coup that she'd made it to the couch. She'd seen the best of Cain the night before when he'd talked Billy into going home and even paid for the ice cream to take to his mother. Yet she knew he didn't see any goodness in himself. And because of that he couldn't forgive himself for the mistakes in their marriage. And because he couldn't forgive himself, he was letting her go. Freeing her.

She loved him with her whole heart and soul but if he didn't want her, then maybe it was time she got the message. She couldn't go on always being alone. Ellie dated. Her friends had gotten married. Yet she was still mourning a marriage that was over.

A soft rap on her door got her head off the back of the sofa. She didn't intend to answer it, but the knock sounded again. This time stronger.

Whoever it was wasn't going away, so she might as well answer. Rising from the sofa, she wrapped herself in her security blanket. When she reached the door, she tugged the soft fleece more securely around herself before she grabbed the knob and opened the door.

Cain smiled at her. "You know, last night when I got home I thought about the things I said when I was counseling Billy, and it occurred to me that I was actually pretty good at talking to people." He pulled in a breath. "Everybody but you."

She snorted a laugh.

"So I'm going to give this a shot. This past week, I've hated myself for being such a terrible husband to you."

"Oh, Cain!"

"Let me finish. I really let you down and I had

every right to be angry with myself. But I also can't wallow in that."

Hope filled Liz's heart. Could he really be saying what she thought he was saying? She opened the door a little wider and invited him inside. "Why don't we have this discussion inside?"

He walked into her small living room. His eyes took note of the neat and tidy room. He smiled sheepishly at her. "How am I doing so far?"

She laughed. Please, please, please let him be headed in the direction that she thought he was headed. "So far you're doing fairly well."

"Okay, then." He drew in a breath and caught her gaze. "I love you and I want to remarry you. I can't change who I was. But I sure as hell don't intend to be that guy anymore."

"Now you're doing fabulously."

This time he laughed. "I was so miserable, so angry with myself, until I remembered what I said to Billy. Suddenly I realized that just like him I had a chance to move on, but I wouldn't if I didn't stop reaching back to the past. Punishing myself. Wallowing in grief."

"Cain, what I told you wasn't easy news," she whispered, so hopeful her voice rattled with it. "I think you deserved a week of confusion."

"I don't want to lose you because of things that happened in the past. We're different. Different enough that this time we can work this out."

"I think so."

"Good. Because I've got some plans." He tugged on her hand, bringing her against him.

Liz smiled up at him. He gazed down at her. And as always happened when they truly looked at each other, the unhappy six years between his brother's death and the present melted away. He looked young and happy, as he had on the flight from Dallas. His eyes had lost the dull regret they'd worn all through their marriage. He really was *her* Cain.

She couldn't pull her gaze away. Not even when his head began to lower and she knew—absolutely knew in her woman's heart—he was going to kiss her.

His lips met hers as a soft brush. It felt so good to be kissed by him, touched by him, that she kissed him back. For three years of being married to him she'd longed for this. Not the passion they'd had in their six-month long-distance relationship. They'd never lost that. But they had lost the need to be together, to connect. They lost happy, joyful, thankful-to-have-each-other kisses. And that's what this was. A happy kiss. An I'm-glad-I-know-you kiss.

He pulled away slowly. "I swear I will never hurt you again."

"I know." Tears flooded her eyes but she blinked them away. This was not the time for tears. Not even happy tears. "So where do you think we should start with this new relationship of ours?"

"At the beginning." He turned her in the direction of her bedroom. "How about if I make you something to eat while you get dressed? Then we can go out on the boat for a while? Just like normal people dating."

"Dating?"

"It's a little something people who like each

other do to see if they should be married or not. It's a step we seemed to have missed."

She laughed. "All right."

He made lunch. Cheese sandwiches and soup. She changed into shorts and a tank top and they went out on the ocean for the rest of the day. The next weekend and every weekend after that for the next six months, they worked on A Friend Indeed houses during the day and attended Cain's myriad social engagements at night. They spent Christmas with her mother and sisters in Philadelphia and New Year's with his parents in Kansas.

When they returned on January second, he lured her back down the hall to his office and sat her on the edge of his desk.

Laughing, she waited while he opened the bottom drawer of his desk and pulled out a jeweler's box. "Open it."

Obedient, but cautious since he'd already given her a Christmas present, she lifted the lid on the little box and her eyes widened. The diamond on the engagement ring inside was huge.

"This is too big!"

He laughed. "In the crowd we run in five carats is about average size."

"The crowd *we* run in is very different from the crowd *you* ran in. We have all kinds of friends now. But I like the ring." She peeked at him. "I'm going to keep it."

"Is that a yes?"

"I don't recall you actually asking me a question."

He got down on one knee and caught her fingers. "Will you marry me?"

Unable to believe this was really happening, she pressed her lips together to keep herself from crying before she said, "On two conditions."

"I'm listening."

"We have a real wedding."

He nodded his agreement.

"And we stay who we are."

He grinned. "I sort of like who we are."

She laughed. Her heart sang with joy that communication could be so easy between them. That they could say so much with so few words, and that they really were getting a second chance.

"Then you are one lucky guy."

He stood up, bent down and kissed her. "You better believe it."

He broke the kiss and Liz noticed an odd-shaped manila envelope stuffed with bubble wrap in the drawer. She kicked it with the toe of her sandal. "What's that?"

"I don't know."

Cain sat on his desk chair and reached down to lift out the fat envelope. He pulled out the bubble wrap and unwound it.

"That's gotta be from your dad. He's the only person I know who goes overboard with bubble wrap."

Cain laughed, but when he finished unwinding, he found the family photo his dad had sent him the weekend Liz had come back into his life.

"What is it?"

He inclined his head, waiting for sadness to

overwhelm him. It didn't. "It's my family's last picture together."

She plucked it from his hands. "Very nice. But your sister looks like a reject from a punk band."

He laughed. "I know."

She turned and set the photo in front of his desk blotter. "I think it should go right here. Right where you can see it every day and be thankful you have such a great family."

Cain smiled. She'd turned his life around in the past few months. She'd brought him out of his shell, got him working for a charity and made him happy when he wasn't really sure he could ever be happy again.

How could he argue with success? Especially when she'd said she'd marry him. Again.

"I think you're right."

EPILOGUE

CAIN AND LIZ'S wedding day the following June turned out to be one of the hottest in Miami's history, making Liz incredibly glad she'd chosen a strapless gown.

On the edge of a canal, in the backyard of the Brill mansion, they toasted their future among family and friends this time. Liz's mom and sisters finally met Cain's parents and sister. The two families blended together as if they'd known each other forever.

Cain's parents were overjoyed that he'd gotten involved in A Friend Indeed and loved that the board of directors from the group *and* many of the women the charity had helped attended the wedding.

Though Liz's mom was happy to see Liz remarrying the man she'd always loved, she was more proud of her daughter's successful business. Her sisters were bridesmaids with Ellie and Amanda. Billy, the surprise best man, lived up to the role with a funny and sentimental toast to the two people who helped him grow from a boy with little to no prospects for the future to a guy who now believed the sky was the limit.

When it was finally time, Cain whisked Liz away. Driving with the top down in "their" beloved Porsche, he took a few turns and got them on the road to his house.

"Why are we going back to the house?"

"It's a surprise."

Wind blowing her veil in a stream behind her, she laughed. "Do we have time for this?"

"It's not like the pilot's going to leave without us, since he has no other passengers." He snuck a glance at her. "Plus, I sign his paycheck."

"True enough." She laughed again and within minutes they were at Cain's front door.

"Is this surprise bigger than a bread box?" she asked as he opened the door and led her inside.

"You'll see." He directed her up the steps.

Raising her full tulle skirt, she raced ahead eager to see what he'd done. "I knew there was a reason you only wanted to sleep at my condo these past few weeks."

"Here I thought I'd pulled a fast one on you."

She turned around and placed a smacking kiss on his lips. "Not hardly."

He laughed and pointed her in the direction of one of his empty bedrooms. He opened the door for her and let her walk inside.

"Oh, Cain!" Staring at the beautiful nursery she could hardly take it all in. "Did you do this?"

"I hired a designer."

"It's gorgeous." She faced him. "But we're not...well, you know. We're not pregnant."

He pulled her into his arms. "I know. I just don't ever want there to be any doubt in your mind again that I'm with you this time. A hundred percent. I want little girls with your eyes and little boys to take fishing."

He kissed her and what started off as something slow and dreamy quickly became hot and steamy.

Just when she thought he'd lower them to the floor, he whispered in her ear, "We have a perfectly good shower in the master suite. We can kill two birds with one stone."

"Two birds?"

"Yeah, we can make love and take a shower before we change into clothes to wear on the trip to Europe."

"I thought we were supposed to change on the plane."

He nibbled her neck. "Plans change."

"And Dale won't mind?"

"Dale is a very patient, understanding man."

He swept her off her feet and carried her to their bedroom, while she undid his tie. He set her down and she tossed his tie to the dresser, as he unzipped her dress. It puddled on the floor and she stepped out of it.

She stood before him in her white lace bra and panties and he sucked in a breath. "You're beautiful."

She kissed him before undoing the buttons of his shirt. "You're not so bad yourself."

He finished undressing and carried her to the shower.

And Dale the pilot got comfortable on the sofa in the office in the hangar housing Cain's private plane, smiling because he had a sneaking feeling he knew why his boss and his new bride had been delayed.

* * * * *